The
Lemonade
Crime

The Lemonade Crime

by
Jacqueline
Davies

Houghton Mifflin Books for Children
Houghton Mifflin Harcourt
Boston New York

ACKNOWLEDGMENTS

Many thanks to the good people who helped shepherd this book: Tracey Adams, Mary Atkinson, Henry Davies, Mae Davies, Tracey Fern, Jennifer Jacobson, Sarah Lamstein, Carol Peacock, and Dana Walrath. A special thanks to Ann Rider, who knew when to push and when to step back—and then push again.

Text copyright © 2011 by Jacqueline Davies
Illustrations by Cara Llewellyn
Pronunciations are reproduced by permission from
The American Heritage Dictionary of the English Language

Houghton Mifflin Books for Children is an imprint of Houghton Mifflin Harcourt Publishing Company.

www.hmhbooks.com

The text of this book is set in Guardi
The illustrations are pen and ink

Library of Congress Cataloging-in-Publication Data
Davies, Jacqueline, 1962–
The lemonade crime / written by Jacqueline Davies.
p. cm.
Summary: When money disappears from fourth-grader Evan's pocket and everyone thinks that his annoying classmate Scott stole it, Evan's younger sister stages a trial involving the entire class, trying to prove what happened.
ISBN 978-0-547-27967-1
[1. Trials—Fiction. 2. Behavior—Fiction. 3. Brothers and sisters—Fiction. 4. Schools—Fiction. 5. Forgiveness—Fiction.] I. Title.
PZ7.D29392Le 2011   [Fic]—dc22   2010015231

Manufactured in the USA
DOC 10 9 8 7 6 5 4
4500402831

For C. Ryan Joyce
in loco parentis to many—
and one, in particular

Contents

Chapter 1
Fraud

fraud (frôd), *n.* The crime of deceiving someone for personal or financial gain; a person who pretends to be something that he or she is not.

"No fair!" said Jessie. She pointed to the four chocolate chip cookies that her brother, Evan, was stuffing into a Ziploc bag. They were standing in the kitchen, just about ready to go to school—the fourth day of fourth grade for both of them, now that they were in the same class.

"Fine," said Evan, taking out one cookie and putting it back in the cookie jar. "Three for you. Three for me. Happy?"

"It's not about being happy," said Jessie. "It's about being fair."

"Whatever. I'm outta here." Evan slung his backpack over his shoulder, then disappeared down the stairs that led to the garage.

Jessie walked to the front-room window and watched as her brother pedaled down the street on his bike. She still didn't have her bike license, so she wasn't allowed to ride to school without a parent riding along. That was just one of the bad things about skipping third grade and being the youngest kid in the fourth-grade class. Everyone else in her class could ride to school, but she still had to walk.

Jessie went to the refrigerator and crossed off another day on the lunch calendar. Today's lunch was Chicken Patty on a Bun. Not her favorite, but okay. With her finger, she tapped each remaining day of the week and read out loud the main dish: Deli-Style Hot Dog (*barf*); Baked Chicken Nuggets with Dipping Sauce; Soft-Shell Tacos; and, on Friday, her favorite: Cinnamon-Glazed French Toast Sticks.

Saturday's box was empty, but someone had used a red marker to fill in the box:

Jessie put her hands on her hips. Who had done that? Probably one of Evan's friends. Adam or Paul. Messing up her lunch calendar. Probably Paul! That was just like him. Jessie knew that Yom Kippur was a very serious Jewish holiday. She couldn't remember what it was for, but it was definitely serious. You were *not* supposed to write the word *par-tay!* after Yom Kippur.

"Jessie, are you all ready?" asked Mrs. Treski, walking into the kitchen.

"Yep," said Jessie. She picked up her backpack, which weighed almost as much as she did, and hefted it onto her shoulders. She had to lean forward slightly at the waist just to keep from falling backwards. "Mom, you don't have to walk me to school anymore. I mean, I'm a fourth-grader, you know?"

"I know you are," said Mrs. Treski, looking on the garage stairs for her shoes. "But you're still just eight years old—"

"I'll be nine next month!"

Mrs. Treski looked at her. "Do you mind so much?"

"Can't I just go with Megan?"

"Isn't Megan always late?"

"But I'm always early, so we'll even out."

"I suppose that would be okay for tomorrow. But today, let's just walk together. Okay?"

"Okay," said Jessie, who actually liked walking to school with her mother, but wondered if the other kids thought she was even more of a weirdo because of it. "But this is the last time."

It took them less than ten minutes to get to school. Darlene, the crossing guard, held up her gloved hands to stop the traffic and called out, "Okay, you can cross now."

Jessie turned to her mother. "Mom, I can walk the rest of the way myself."

"Well," said Mrs. Treski, one foot on the curb, one foot in the street. "All right. I'll see you when school gets out. I'll wait for you right here." She stepped back up on the curb, and Jessie knew she was watching her all the way to the playground. *I won't turn around and wave,* she told herself. *Fourth-graders don't do that kind of thing.* Evan had explained that to her.

Jessie walked onto the playground, looking for Megan. Kids weren't allowed in the school building until the bell rang, so they gathered outside before school, hanging on the monkey bars, sliding down the slide, talking in groups, or organizing a quick game of soccer or basketball—if they were lucky enough to have a teacher who would let them borrow a class ball before school. Jessie scanned the whole playground. No Megan. She was probably running late.

Jessie hooked her thumbs under the straps of her backpack. She had already noticed that most of the fourth grade girls didn't carry backpacks. They carried their books and binders and water bottles and lunches in slouchy mailbags. Jessie thought those bags were stupid, the way they banged against your knees and dug into your shoulder. Backpacks were more practical.

She wandered toward the blacktop where Evan and a bunch of boys were playing HORSE. Some of the boys were fifth-graders and tall, but Jessie wasn't surprised to find out that Evan was winning. He was good at basketball. The best in his whole grade, in Jessie's opinion. Maybe even the best in the whole school. She sat down on the sidelines to watch.

"Okay, I'm gonna do a fadeaway jumper," said Evan, calling his shot so the next boy would have to copy him. "One foot on the short crack to start." He bounced the ball a few times, and Jessie watched along with all the other kids to see if he could make the shot. When he finally jumped, releasing the ball as he fell back, the ball sailed through the air and made a perfect rainbow—right through the hoop.

"Oh, man!" said Ryan, who had to copy the shot. He bounced the ball a couple of times and bent his knees, but just then the bell rang and it was time to line up. "Ha!" said Ryan, throwing the ball sky high.

"You are so lucky," said Evan, grabbing the ball out of the air and putting it in the milk crate that held the rest of the 4-O playground equipment.

Jessie liked Evan's friends, and they were usually pretty nice to her, so she followed them to stand in line. She knew not to get in line right behind Evan. He wasn't too thrilled about having his little sister in the same classroom with him this year. Mrs. Treski had given Jessie some advice: *Give Evan some space,* so that's what she was doing.

Jessie looked across the playground just in case Megan had appeared, but instead she saw Scott Spencer jumping out of his dad's car. "Oh, great!" muttered Jessie. As far as Jessie was concerned, Scott Spencer was a faker and a fraud. He was always doing something he wasn't supposed to behind the teacher's back, and he never got caught. Like the time he cut the heads off the daffodils that were growing in the art room. Or when he erased stars from the blackboard so that his desk group would win the weekly Team Award.

When Scott got to the line, he cut right in front of Jessie and tapped Ryan on the back of the shoulder. "Hey," he said.

"Hey," said Ryan, turning and giving him a nod.

"Excuse me," said Jessie, poking Scott in the arm. "The end of the line is back there." She jerked her thumb behind her.

"So what?" said Scott.

"So you can't just cut in front."

"Who cares? All we're doing is going into school."

"It's a line," said Jessie. "The rule is you go to the end of the line."

"Who cares what you say?" said Scott, shrugging and turning his back on her. The line was starting to move forward. Scott punched a couple more boys on the arm and said hey to them. Some of the boys said hi back, but Jessie noticed that Evan kept looking straight ahead.

"Man, am I late," said Scott to Ryan. He was grinning from ear to ear. "I couldn't stop playing my new Xbox 20/20."

"You got a 20/20?" asked Ryan.

Paul turned around. "Who did? Who got one?"

"He says he did," said Ryan, pointing to Scott.

"No way," said Paul. "That's not even out yet."

"Well, you can't get it in a store," said Scott. "But my mom knows people in Japan."

Jessie looked toward Evan, who was at the front of the line. She could tell that he hadn't heard what Scott said, but more and more boys in line turned around to hear about the 20/20. It was the newest game system, with surround-sight goggles and motion-sensing gloves. The line in front of Jessie started to bunch up.

When Jessie got to the door of her classroom, Mrs. Overton was standing there, saying good morning to each student as the line filed in.

"Mrs. Overton, Scott Spencer cut in front of me this morning." Jessie was no tattletale, but Scott needed to learn a thing or two about rules.

Mrs. Overton put a hand on Jessie's shoulder. "Okay, Jessie. I'll watch tomorrow to make sure it doesn't happen again, but for now, let's just let it go."

Perfect! thought Jessie as she walked to her desk and took down her chair. *Scott Spencer gets away with something again.*

After putting her chair on the floor, she walked out into the hall to hang her backpack in her locker. She tore off a corner of a page from her Writer's Notebook and quickly wrote a note on it. Then, as she passed Evan's desk on the way to her own, she slipped the note into his hand. She didn't see him open it and read it, but by the time she sat down at her own desk, she could tell that he had. Evan was staring at Scott Spencer, and you could practically see bullets coming out of his eyes.

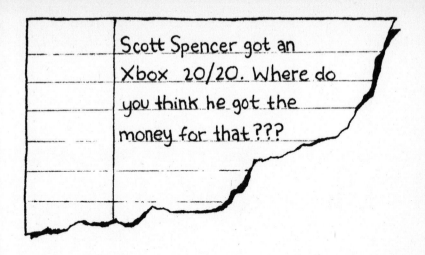

Scott Spencer got an
Xbox 20/20. Where do
you think he got the
money for that???

Chapter 2
Revenge

revenge (rǐ-věnj′), *n.* The act of causing pain or harm to another person because that person has injured you in some way.

Evan crushed the note in his hand. Suddenly he didn't feel like laughing and joking around with his friends. Suddenly he wanted to punch his fist through the wall.

Here's why: Evan was more certain than ever that Scott had stolen money from him. It had happened just last week. Right in the middle of that heat wave. Right in the middle of the lemonade war with Jessie. They'd all been at Jack's house. All the guys—Paul and Ryan and Kevin and Malik and Scott—were playing pool basketball. Evan had $208 in the pocket of his shorts. *Two hundred and eight dollars!* It was more money than he'd ever seen in his whole life. He'd left his shorts folded on the bed in Jack's bedroom while they all went swimming. But then Scott got out of the pool to go to the bathroom. And a minute later, he came running out of the house, saying he had to go home right away. And when Evan went back in the house to get dressed, the money was gone.

It had been the worst feeling in Evan's entire life.

Once upon a time, about a million years ago, Scott and Evan had been friends. Sort of. Evan used to play at Scott's house a lot, and once in a while Scott would play at Evan's, although Scott said his house was better because there was more stuff to do. One time, Evan even went overnight to Scott's beach house on the Cape. The Spencers had plenty of money because Scott's mom was a lawyer at one of the biggest law offices downtown and his dad ran a financial consulting business out of their home.

But things had cooled off since then. Way off. The truth was, Scott was kind of a pain to be around.

The way he bragged, the way he cheated at games, even stupid little games like Go Fish or Operation. Who cared about winning a game like Go Fish? And the way he kept things locked up—like the snacks at his house! He kept Yodels and Ring Dings locked in a metal file cabinet in his basement. If Evan thought about it, he had to admit that he really couldn't stand the kid. And now he had a reason to hate him.

"Morning work, Evan," said Mrs. Overton, tapping the work sheet on his desk as she walked by. Evan turned back to his own desk and studied the Daily Double math problem in front of him. All the other kids in the class were working on the same problem, and Evan could tell that some of them had already finished. Normally this would have made him tense, but this morning, he couldn't even concentrate enough on the problem to get that *uh-oh* feeling inside of him.

I'd get an Xbox. The new one. That's what Scott had said last week, just before the money disappeared from Evan's shorts. They were trying to figure out how much money they would make from a lemonade stand and what they would buy if they got rich. Suddenly rich.

And now he had an Xbox. Scott Spencer had a 20/20, and Evan was sure he'd bought it with the money he'd stolen from Evan's pocket. Evan felt like lifting his head and howling.

Sh-sh-sh-sh-sh-sh-sh. A sound like a rattlesnake ready to strike shimmied through the classroom. Evan looked up. Mrs. Overton was shaking the big African *shekere* she used to get everyone's attention. The beads draped around the hollowed-out gourd made a rustling, rattling sound.

"Okay, Paper Collectors," said Mrs. Overton, "please gather the Daily Doubles and put them on my desk." Every week, the students in 4-O were assigned a job. Some of the jobs were serious, like Paper Collector and Equipment Manager and Attendance Monitor, and some of them were silly, like Chicken Dresser (the person who chose an outfit for the rubber chicken that sat on Mrs. Overton's desk) and Goofy Face Maker (the person who made a face that all the kids in 4-O had to copy at the end of the day on Friday). "Everyone else, come over to the rug for Morning Meeting."

Evan looked back down at the blank math problem in front of him. The only thing he'd written on his page was his name. He handed the paper to Sarah Monroe, then walked over to the rug in the corner and dropped onto the floor, his back up against the bookcase.

"Evan, sit up, please," said Mrs. Overton, smiling at him. "No slouching in the circle." Evan crossed his legs and sat up properly.

First, they went around the circle and every person had to say hello to the person on the right and the person on the left, but in a different way. When it was his turn, Evan said *"konichiwa"* to Adam, who was sitting next to him. Evan liked saying the Japanese word. It made him feel like he was kicking a ball around inside his mouth. Jessie used sign language to say hello to Megan. Scott Spencer said "Whassup?" to Ryan, which made everyone in the class laugh. Everyone except Evan.

Then Mrs. Overton turned to a fresh page on the

Morning Board. A wild goose had landed on the playground yesterday morning, and that was the topic for discussion. Mrs. Overton wanted to know what the kids knew about geese in particular and migrating birds in general. So they took turns until every single one of them had written a fact on the easel. Evan wrote, *Some birds fly for days.* He was going to add *when they migrate,* but he was pretty sure he'd mess up the spelling of the word *migrate,* so he left off that part.

When they'd finished talking about geese and migration, Mrs. Overton capped the Magic Markers and said, "Would anyone like to share something with the class before we go back to our desks?" About half the kids raised their hand, but no one's hand went up faster than Scott Spencer's.

"Scott?" said Mrs. Overton. Evan slumped back against the bookcase. He did not want to hear what Scott had to share with the class.

"I got an Xbox 20/20," Scott said, looking around at all the other kids.

Immediately, the class exploded with noise.

Twenty-seven fourth-graders started talking at once. Mrs. Overton had to shake her *shekere* for nearly ten seconds to get the kids to quiet down.

"Holy rubber chickens!" said Mrs. Overton. The kids in 4-O laughed. "I can tell you're all interested in Scott's new game box. Let's have three questions for Scott about his share, and then we'll move on to the next person."

Mrs. Overton called on Alyssa first.

"What's so great about a 20/20?" she asked.

"Are you kidding?" said Paul. "You put on these goggles, and the TV goes totally 3-D."

"Paul, remember to raise your hand if you want to talk," said Mrs. Overton.

Scott nodded his head. "Yeah, it's like you're really *in* the jungle," said Scott. "Or in a car chase. Or wherever the game goes. And the controls are the gloves you wear. It's how you move your fingers, like this." Scott held out his hands and showed how he moved them in different ways to make things happen in the game. Ryan shook his head as if he couldn't quite believe it.

Mrs. Overton looked at all the hands that were still raised. "Question number two? Jack?"

"What games do you have?" asked Jack. All the boys and even some of the girls had turned their bodies so that the whole circle was facing Scott.

"So far I've got Defenders, Road Rage, and Crisis. And then I've got a whole bunch that are in Japanese, and I have no idea what they are."

The class started to whisper and talk again until Mrs. Overton called for the last question before moving on. "Jessie?"

Evan sat up a little, wondering what his little sister would ask. The first few days of school, Jessie had hardly said a word. Now everyone in the class turned to hear what she had to say.

"How much did it cost?" she asked.

Evan smiled. Leave it to Jessie to ask the one thing that everyone wanted to know but didn't dare ask.

"Jessie, that's not an appropriate question," said Mrs. Overton.

Jessie's forehead wrinkled up. "Why not?"

"We don't talk about money in class," said Mrs. Overton.

"We do in math," said Jessie. "All the time."

"That's different," said Mrs. Overton. "What I mean is, we don't ask each other how much things cost. It isn't polite. Okay, let's move on. Evan, do you have something you'd like to share with the class?"

Evan had raised his hand, and now he dropped it. "Since Jessie's question didn't count, can I ask the third question?"

Mrs. Overton paused for a minute. Evan could tell that she wanted to move on to a different topic, but she also wanted to follow the rules of Morning Meeting. "Okay," she said. "That seems fair."

Evan turned to Scott and looked him right in the face. That feeling came over him, the same one he'd had when he read Jessie's note. It was like a giant steamroller. Evan almost never got angry or jealous, but now he wanted to reach across the room and grab Scott and shake something out of him.

"Who bought it?" he asked. "You or your parents?"

Scott jutted his chin out, like he did when he was challenging Evan on the basketball court. "*I* did. All my own money."

The class erupted again, and Mrs. Overton didn't bother with the *shekere*. She just held her hands up and said, "4-O!" When they quieted down, she said, "Scott, it's very impressive that you saved your money for something you wanted to buy. Now let's move on."

But Evan couldn't move on. He couldn't listen to Salley tell the class about the trip she'd taken to her grandparents' house. Or even to Paul talk about the nest of snakes he'd found in his backyard. He couldn't hear anything or see anything. That feeling was all over him, through him, inside him. That feeling of wanting to shake something out of Scott. And now he knew what it was he wanted.

Evan wanted revenge.

Chapter 3
Eyewitness

eyewitness (ī′wĭt′nĭs), *n.* A person who actually sees something happen and so can give a first-person account of the event.

Jessie stood in the doorway, one foot inside the classroom, one foot outside on the playground. All the other kids had run outside. Everyone except Evan and Megan. They were staying inside to finish their Daily Double.

Jessie didn't want to go outside if Megan and Evan weren't there. She still didn't know most of the fourth-graders—not enough to know who was friendly and who wasn't—and she knew she'd probably say the wrong thing to the wrong person. And people would laugh. Or be mean. Or just give her one of those looks—those looks she never understood—and then turn their backs on her.

Maybe Jessie could stay inside and read her Independent Reading book instead. It was worth asking.

She walked back to her desk and pulled out *The Prince and the Pauper*. It was a book her grandmother had given to her. Twice, actually. First, Grandma sent it at the beginning of the summer with a note that said, *Jessie, I loved this book when I was your age.* Then a month later she'd sent another copy of the same book with a note that said, *This book made me think of you, Jessie. Hope you enjoy it!*

Jessie had laughed and said, "I hope she forgets and sends me my birthday money twice!" But Mrs. Treski didn't laugh. She frowned and shook her head and went to the phone to give her mother a call, just to see how she was doing.

"Mrs. Overton?" said Jessie. Evan had gone to the boys' room, and Megan was in the hall getting a drink of water, so the room was empty except for Jessie and her teacher.

"Yes, Jessie?" Mrs. Overton looked up from her desk, where she was reading over what the students had written in their Writer's Notebooks that morning. Jessie had written about the fireworks that she and Evan and her mother had watched from their house on Labor Day. She'd used lots of long words, like *kaleidoscope* and *panorama,* and vigorous verbs, like *exploded* and *cascading.* She thought her paragraph was pretty good.

Jessie heard Evan and Megan laughing in the hallway. That stopped her, the way they were laughing together. She didn't want them to see her, staying inside with the teacher during recess. She was pretty sure that Evan would say, "That's not what fourth-graders do." So she mumbled, "Uh, nothing," and carried her book back to her desk.

"You should go outside, honey," said Mrs. Overton. "You don't want to miss all of morning recess. Right?"

"Right," said Jessie faintly. She hurried to the back door, the one that opened right onto the playground. When she turned to close the door behind her, she saw Evan and Megan walking into the classroom from the hallway. They both looked pretty happy, considering that they were missing recess *and* had to do math.

Outside, a handful of girls were sitting at the picnic table, folding origami flowers. Some of the fourth-graders were swinging and sliding on the Green Machine. About eight or nine were playing kickball. All of Evan's friends—Paul and Ryan and Adam and Jack—were shooting baskets, along with Scott Spencer. Where should Jessie go? She wondered if the boys were still talking about the 20/20 so she drifted over to the basketball hoop. She sat down on the grass and pretended to concentrate on her book, but really she was listening to the boys' conversation. Jessie overheard Paul ask Scott, "How'd you save up that much?" They weren't playing a real game, just shooting free throws from the line.

"Lots of ways," said Scott. Paul bounce-passed the ball to Scott, and he took his shot. And missed. Jessie was glad to see that.

"Like what?" asked Adam.

"I did a lot of chores around the house."

"There's no way you saved up that much money from doing chores," said Adam.

"I did, too," said Scott. Now he held on to the ball and dribbled it in place. Ryan held up his hands for it—it was his turn to shoot—but Scott wouldn't give it up. "What're you saying?"

"I'm saying what I said," said Adam. "There's no *way* you saved up that much money just from chores."

What he's saying, thought Jessie, *is that you stole all our lemonade money from Evan, and everybody knows it!* If only someone had seen him take it. If only there'd been an eyewitness—like the crime shows on TV! Then Scott wouldn't have gotten off . . . scot-free.

A shadow fell across the page of her book. Jessie looked up, and there was David Kirkorian standing next to her.

Jessie still didn't know a lot of the fourth-graders, but David Kirkorian was legendary throughout the school. Everyone said he had all kinds of weird collections at his house. He kept a jar of peach pits on his dresser, and he added a new one every time he ate a peach. He had a box full of shoelaces from every shoe he'd ever worn. He even had a large brown envelope filled with his own toenail clippings. At least, that's what everybody said, though Jessie was pretty sure that no one had actually seen the envelope.

"You're not allowed to read outside during recess," said David.

"I never heard of that rule," said Jessie.

"Just because you don't know a rule doesn't mean it isn't a rule." David started picking at one of his fingernails, and Jessie wondered if he collected those, too.

"That's the dumbest rule I ever heard."

"No, it's not," said David. "You could get run over sitting here. You're not even paying attention. A ball could conk you on the head. You could *die.*"

He started to walk off in the direction of the duty teacher. Jessie felt her face getting hot. What was David going to say to the duty teacher?

Jessie stood up and hurried toward the school building. She would say that she had a stomachache. She would go to the nurse. Mrs. Graham always let you lie down for a couple of minutes before sending you back to your class. It was a good place to rest and be quiet. A good place to think. And Jessie had a lot of thinking to do. Not just about rules and recess. But about how unfair it was that Scott always escaped punishment—and what she could do to change that.

"Toenail collector," Jessie muttered under her breath as she hurried inside.

Chapter 4
Hearsay

hearsay (hîr′sā′), *n.* Quoting someone else's words when that person is not present to say whether those words are true; rumor. Hearsay is not allowed as evidence in a court of law.

"So, you get it?" asked Megan, leaning back in her chair. "They're the same. See?"

The math problem was about symmetry. There were five different shapes drawn on the page, and for each one, Evan had to figure out if the shape was symmetrical or not. If it was, he had to draw the line of symmetry. Megan had already done the first one to show him how.

But Evan was having a hard time thinking about symmetry when he was sitting right next to Megan Moriarty.

"That one's easy," said Evan, trying to sound cool. "Everybody knows that hearts are symmetric."

"Not all hearts," said Megan. "Look at this one."

"Well, that's just freaky," said Evan.

The next three shapes weren't too hard, and Evan was able to draw the line of symmetry for each one.

But the last one had him stumped, and Megan finally had to let him in on the trick: the shape wasn't symmetrical at all.

"It looks like it should work," said Megan, "but it never does, no matter where you draw the line. Jessie showed me that. She's a math genius, huh?"

Evan didn't say anything. Having a sister who was smart enough to skip a whole grade was like having a best friend who was a basketball star. It made you look bad by comparison.

"Hey, Evan?" said Megan, dropping her voice and leaning in even closer. They both looked over at Mrs. Overton, who was talking on the class phone. Evan could smell the coconut shampoo Megan used on her hair. It made him think of ice cream at the Big Dipper. "How do *you* think Scott Spencer got the money for that 20/20?"

The nice, floaty feeling leaked out of Evan. "Scott Spencer? Huh!" said Evan.

"I know what you mean," said Megan, sitting back and twirling her hair. "He always acts so nice when the teacher's around, but then he's really mean in the halls."

"Yeah, that's Scott," mumbled Evan.

"You know," said Megan, leaning in again. "Scott once told me his mother makes ten dollars a *minute.* Do you believe that?"

Evan thought of the Spencers' house and the vacations they took every year—skiing and the Caribbean and even Europe—and he didn't doubt it for a second. "Sure," he said. "You should see where he lives."

"I heard he has a new TV that's as big as the whiteboard." Megan pointed to the large whiteboard at the front of the room.

"Probably," said Evan. "You wouldn't think a kid like that would steal things."

Megan's eyes opened wide. "Does he really steal? Alyssa told me he does. She said he took her charm bracelet out of her locker and then pretended he'd found it on the playground. Just to impress her. But I don't know if that's true."

Evan was dying to tell her that Scott had stolen

$208 from him—but he couldn't. "He stole lunch money from Ryan once. And he took a candy bar from the Price Chopper. He steals lots of things."

Megan looked at him closely. "Did you see him take the money or the candy bar?" she asked.

Evan shook his head. "No, but Ryan said—"

"That's just a rumor, then," said Megan. "You can't believe everything you hear. That's what my parents always say."

"If you knew him like I do, you'd think it was true, too."

"Maybe," said Megan. "But I don't listen to rumors. People probably say things about me that aren't true! And about you, too!"

Evan wondered if that was so. What would people say about him? Did his friends talk about him behind his back? He didn't like to think about that.

But what Megan said got him thinking about the missing money. Evan never actually saw Scott take the money, but he had told everyone—Paul and Ryan and Adam and Jack—that Scott had taken it.

And they'd all believed him, because . . . well, because it was true! Evan was sure of it.

"You have to know Scott," Evan said, shaking his head again. But he could hear his mother's voice: *Rumors are like pigeons. They fly everywhere and make a mess wherever they go.*

Chapter 5
Accused

accused (ə-kyōōzd'), *n.* A person who has been charged with a crime or who is on trial for a crime.

Jessie and Megan were walking to school, and they were late. Jessie had called Megan at 7:00 that morning, and again at 7:30, and then at 7:55 *and* 8:10, but Megan had still been late leaving her house. ("I was late because you kept calling me," she grumbled on the way out the door.) *Ten whole minutes late.* So now they were half running, half walking, trying to get to school before the bell rang.

Normally, Jessie wouldn't have minded missing the before-school time on the playground, but today she had things to do. On the playground. Before school. With no grownups around.

"C'mon, c'mon," she said to Megan. Megan's legs were longer than Jessie's, but Megan was slow because her mailbag kept banging into her knees.

"Why do we need to get there so early?" asked Megan. She was loping along, about ten feet behind Jessie.

"You'll see when we get there. Keep running, keep running."

"Better hurry, girls," said Darlene when they got to the crosswalk. "I heard the first bell." Jessie and Megan speed-walked across the street. Running wasn't allowed.

"Oh, no!" said Jessie when they rounded the corner and caught sight of the playground. "They're already lining up. Come *on!*"

By the time Jessie and Megan ran onto the blacktop, the entire fourth grade was lined up, waiting for the signal to file into school. The girls should have gone to the end of the line, but Jessie marched right up to the middle, where Scott Spencer was trying to knock Paul's baseball cap off his head. Evan was standing farther up, bouncing the class basketball. He was Equipment Manager this week, which meant he was responsible for bringing in all the playground stuff—balls, jump ropes, Frisbees.

"Hey," said Scott, noticing Jessie. "The end of the line is back *there!*"

"So?" said Jessie, rummaging in her backpack.

"So no cutting," said Scott. "Isn't that the *rule?*" Even Jessie could tell he was making fun of her.

"I'm not cutting," said Jessie, pulling a piece of paper from her backpack and holding it out in front of her. "I'm serving you with a warrant for your arrest."

A few of the boys in front of Scott turned around, and some of the girls at the end of the line moved up so they could see, too.

"You're what?" asked Scott.

"Here, take it," said Jessie, shoving the piece of paper closer to him. Scott reached out and grabbed it like he was going to rip it to shreds.

"That's it!" shouted Jessie. "You touched it. That

means you've been served. Now you have to appear in court." Jessie was pretty sure she knew what she was doing. She had been reading a booklet called "Trial by Jury: The American Legal System in a Nutshell." It was one of the public service booklets that her mom wrote as part of her business as a public relations consultant.

Scott immediately dropped the paper on the ground like it was on fire. "You can't do that!"

"Oh, yes I can," said Jessie. "If you touch it, that means you've been served. You can't get out of it now."

"Get out of what? What are you even talking about?" By now, everyone in the line had turned to watch. Evan had stopped dribbling the basketball, but he didn't leave his spot in line.

Jessie picked up the arrest warrant from the ground and read it out loud. She had written it using the calligraphy pen her grandmother had given her for her last birthday.

Warrant for the Arrest of
Scott Spencer

Scott Spencer, you are hereby charged with the crime of stealing $208 from the pocket of Evan Treski's shorts on September 5th of this year.

On Friday, you are to appear in court to plead your case. There, a jury of your peers will decide if you are guilty or not. If you are found guilty, your punishment

She got as far as that when Scott interrupted.

"You gotta be kidding me," he said, crossing his arms and laughing. "You're joking, right?"

Jessie shook her head. Not a single person in the fourth-grade line was talking. Everyone was watching Jessie and Scott. She continued reading, "'If you are found guilty—'"

41

"Are you saying," said Scott, his eyes narrowing and a scowl appearing on his face, "that I stole money?"

Jessie took a deep breath. She knew it was a big deal to accuse someone like that.

"Yes, I am," she said. There were murmurs among the fourth-graders.

"What about *you?*" asked Scott, turning toward Evan and taking a few steps forward. He reached out to poke Evan in the chest, but Evan swatted his hand away before it ever touched him. "Are *you* saying I stole your money?"

Jessie looked at Evan. He dribbled the basketball twice, then held it in his hand, staring at it. Suddenly, Jessie realized that she should have talked to Evan before doing any of this. He was the one who'd been the victim of the crime. He was the one who would still have to play with Scott every day at recess. He was the one who would have to testify against him in a court of law.

But it was too late now. Everyone was watching them. Everyone was waiting to see what would happen next.

Evan dribbled the ball again. One, two, three. Jessie knew that he was thinking. Evan thought with his whole body, not just his brain.

"That's what I'm saying," he said quietly. "I'm saying you stole the money from me."

The line of fourth-graders had twisted into the shape of a large, sloppy C with both ends watching what was happening in the middle.

Now that Evan had accused Scott of stealing, the line started to fall apart entirely as kids pulled in close to hear what Scott would say next.

But it was Jessie who spoke first. "'If you are found guilty, your punishment will be that you have to give your new Xbox 20/20 to Evan Treski.'"

"No way!" said Scott, but he could barely be heard over all the noise that the fourth-graders were making. Everyone had an opinion about the fairness of the punishment.

"Hey," said Ryan. "What happens if he's found not guilty?"

Jessie shook her head. "He won't be."

"I will, too, you twerp!" said Scott. "And when I am, here's what's going to happen. Both of you"—he pointed at Jessie and Evan—"are going to stand up in Morning Meeting and tell everyone, including Mrs. Overton, that you told lies about me and that I didn't take anything from anyone. And then you're going to apologize to me. In front of *everyone*."

"4-O!" Mrs. Overton was standing in the doorway, a look of dismay on her face. "What kind of a line is this?"

The kids scrambled back to their places, and those at the front started the morning march into the classroom. But Evan, Jessie, and Scott still faced each other.

"Is it a deal?" asked Scott.

"Deal," said Evan, and turned his back on them to head inside.

"I'll even put it in writing," said Jessie. She waved the arrest warrant in front of Scott. Then she picked up her backpack and hurried to the end of the line, smiling.

Soon, justice would be served.

Agreement of Atonement following the Trial of Scott Spencer

If Scott Spencer is found GUILTY in a court of law of the crime of stealing $208 from the pocket of Evan Treski's shorts on September the 5th of this year, he will give his Xbox 20/20 to Evan Treski to keep forever.

If Scott Spencer is found NOT GUILTY in a court of law of the crime of stealing $208 from the pocket of Evan Treski's shorts on September 5th of this year, Evan and Jessie Treski will stand up in Morning Meeting on Monday and will tell the entire class that Scott Spencer did not steal $208 from the pocket of Evan Treski's shorts on September 5th of this year, and they will apologize to him for telling lies.

Evan Treski

Jessie Treski

Scott Spencer

Chapter 6
Impartial

impartial (ĭm-pär′shǝl), *adj.* Treating everyone the same; not taking sides in an argument; fair and just.

At recess, Jessie didn't waste any time. Evan watched as she pulled index cards, one by one, out of a big envelope. All the fourth-graders crowded around.

"You're the plaintiff," she said to Evan, and handed him a green index card that said PLAINTIFF on it. "That means you're the victim of the crime." Evan studied the card, then stuck it in his back pocket. A kids' court sounded like a crazy idea to him. A crazy Jessie idea. But he was used to those, and this one might get him a new Xbox 20/20, not to mention the satisfaction of proving Scott's guilt in front of everybody. For that, he was willing to give it a try.

"I'm Evan's lawyer," said Jessie, and she gave herself a purple index card that said LAWYER FOR THE PLAINTIFF.

Then she turned to Scott. "You're the defendant, which means you're the one who's on trial." She gave him a yellow index card that said DEFENDANT on it.

Then she started to hand out five orange index cards.

"Hey!" shouted Scott. "Don't I get a lawyer?"

"Hold on! You'll get one in a minute," said Jessie sharply. She continued handing out cards.

"I want Ryan," said Scott.

"Sorry," said Ryan, holding up an orange card. "I'm a witness."

"Then I want Paul."

"He's a witness, too," said Jessie, handing Paul the last orange card. "Everyone who was at Jack's house on the day of the crime is a witness."

"Well, then who's going to be *my* lawyer?" asked Scott, crumpling his DEFENDANT card.

Jessie ignored his question. She held up a purple card. "Megan, you're on the jury," she said. Evan's heart jumped. There was one vote he could count on.

"When's the trial?" said Megan.

"After school," said Jessie. "On Friday."

Megan shook her head. "I think we're going away this weekend."

"You can't miss the trial!" said Jessie. Evan wanted to shout the same thing, but he kept his mouth shut.

"I'll talk to my mom," said Megan. "Maybe we can leave later. But you'd better give this card to somebody else." She handed the purple card back to Jessie.

"Oh, all right," said Jessie, sounding disappointed. "Take one of these." She handed Megan a white card that said AUDIENCE on it.

It only took Jessie another minute to hand out the twelve JURY cards and the rest of the AUDIENCE cards. All the audience members were girls because all the witnesses were boys and the jury, as Jessie explained to everyone, had to be fifty-fifty.

Evan looked around. It was weird, the way all the kids were going along with Jessie's idea. Didn't they know this was all fake? And how did Jessie know all this legal stuff? How did she always know things he didn't know?

Jessie rounded up the six girls who held white audience cards. Then she turned to Scott. "You can pick anybody from the audience to be your lawyer. Technically, we don't even need the audience. No offense," said Jessie, turning to the girls.

"I don't want a girl lawyer," said Scott.

"Suit yourself," said Jessie, shrugging. "But don't come back and complain you weren't offered legal counsel."

"A bunch of girls!" said Scott. "Some offer! I'll be my own lawyer. I'll defend myself." He turned to Jessie. "And I'll beat you at it, too!" he said. That was just like Scott, thought Evan. Always thinking he was the best. Always the kid who had the best stuff. Who took the best vacations. Who had everything.

"Good," said Jessie. "Defend yourself." There was just one more index card in her envelope. Evan watched as she pulled it out slowly. The card was red. It had one word on it.

Jessie looked around like she was making a very important decision, but Evan knew she'd already decided who would get that red card. Jessie never left anything until the last minute.

"The judge is going to be . . . David Kirkorian."

There was dead silence.

Then Paul shouted out, "Are you kidding me?"

"He can't be a judge!" said Ryan. "He collects human bones!"

"I do not!" said David, turning bright red but stepping up to Jessie and taking the card out of her hand.

Then everyone started talking at once. David, meanwhile, held up the red card and shouted, "Ha, ha! I'm the judge! I'm the judge!" They made so much noise, the duty teacher came over to see what was going on with class 4-O. That quieted everyone down. Nobody wanted the duty teacher getting involved. One of the unspoken rules on the playground was *Never tell the duty teacher what's really going on.*

"Why him?" asked Paul after the duty teacher walked away.

"Because he's the only one in the whole class who's *impartial*," said Jessie. "He's not friends with Evan or Scott. He'll be fair. He won't play favorites. And that's the most important thing about a judge. A judge has to treat everyone the same."

David held up the red card in one hand and placed the other one over his heart. "I solemnly swear that I'll be a fair judge," he said.

"Good," said Jessie.

But Evan couldn't believe it. Who was going to listen to a kid like David Kirkorian?

For Evan, the day went downhill from there. All afternoon in class, they worked on things that Evan hated: math fact drills, spelling rules, and writers' workshop. Then Mrs. Overton discovered that one of the jump ropes was missing from the 4-O milk crate, and that was Evan's fault because he was Equipment Manager.

But the thing that really slam-dunked the day right into the garbage can, the thing that changed it from a crummy day into absolutely one of the top ten worst days of his life, happened after school.

Evan was strapping on his bike helmet when Adam walked up to him at the rack and pulled out his bike. "You want to come over?" asked Evan.

"Can't," said Adam. "I promised my mom I'd help her get the house ready for Yom Kippur."

"Is that today?" asked Evan, clicking the buckle under his chin.

"It starts Friday night, but my mom wants me to clean up my room today and do some other stuff, too."

Evan knew that Yom Kippur is a holiday where the grownups don't eat all day. It was supposed to help them think about their sins, but Evan couldn't figure that out. When he was hungry, he couldn't think about anything except what he was going to eat next.

"You want to come to the break-fast party?" asked Adam. The Goldbergs always ate a big meal at sunset when the holiday fast was over.

"Sure," said Evan. He'd been to lots of Friday

night dinners at Adam's and Paul's houses. He liked the candles and even the prayers he didn't understand, but mostly he liked the food: challah bread, roasted chicken, and applesauce cake.

"Are you going to go the whole day without eating this year?" asked Evan. Last year, Adam had bragged that he was going to fast next year for Yom Kippur.

Adam shrugged. "I might try." Then he looked down at his bike and bounced the front wheel a couple of times on the hard blacktop. "Look. Uh. There's something I've been meaning to say to you. You remember how over the summer, Paul and Kevin and me, we ditched you in the woods that time?"

"Yeah," said Evan, wondering why Adam was bringing up something that had happened months ago. Evan had been really mad back then, but now it was over.

"Well, I'm really sorry. And I hope you'll forgive me." Evan looked confused. Adam shrugged. "Dude. It's Yom Kippur. The Day of Atonement. You have to go around and ask people to forgive your sins."

Evan laughed. "You're such an idiot!" He shoved Adam. Adam grinned, faked like he was going to throw a punch, then got on his bike, and rode away.

Evan was just about to push off on his bike when he saw Ryan and Paul walking together toward the path. He rode across the blacktop and crossed in front of them right before they came to the fence. Before Evan could say anything, Paul slung his arm around him, nearly knocking him off his bike. "Hey, Evan, I totally owe you one. Thanks for taking the blame, you know, when Charlie got off his leash."

"Yeah, sure. No big deal," said Evan, shrugging. Evan and Paul did that all the time for each other: swapping the blame so that they wouldn't get in trouble with their own parents. Parents always went way easier on other people's kids than they did on their own.

"You want to come over?" Evan said to Paul and Ryan, balancing on his bike without pedaling forward.

Paul shook his head. "No, we're going to Scott's."

Evan slammed his feet to the ground and stared at the two of them.

"He said we could try out the 20/20," said Ryan. "It's supposed to be awesome. You should come, too."

Evan felt like he'd been sucker-punched. "No way!" he shouted. He stared at Paul and then Ryan with an expression that said, *Traitor!* but neither one of them said anything in return. Finally, Evan said quietly, "I can't believe you're going over to his house."

Paul shrugged. "He didn't do anything to us."

"Some friend you are," said Evan.

"C'mon, Evan," said Paul. "You don't even know for sure that he took the money . . . "

"I know!" said Evan.

"You should come," said Ryan. "Everyone's going over there after school."

A picture came into Evan's mind of the whole fourth-grade class marching over to Scott's house. All his friends. And where would he be? He'd be at home, with his little sister. "Who?" he asked. "Everyone, who?"

"All the guys," said Paul. "You know, me and Ryan and Jack and Kevin. All the guys."

"Not Adam," said Evan, thinking to himself that at least he had one friend who was loyal.

"Well, he's gotta help his mother with some stuff," said Ryan, "but then he's coming over after that. Like in an hour."

Evan shook his head in disbelief. His best friend. Stabbing him in the back. He yanked his handlebars away from Paul and Ryan and rode off without saying another word.

Chapter 7
Due Diligence

due diligence (doo dĭl′ə-jəns), *n*. Taking the time and making the effort to do a reasonably good job at something; the opposite of negligence.

"Can we take a break now?" asked Megan, sitting up on her knees. She held the blue marker in her hand as if it were a lighted candle. Her fingers were covered with ink in all colors, and she had a pencil stuck through the base of her ponytail.

Jessie was lying on her stomach with her whole box of colored pencils spread out in front of her. There was no way they could take a break now! The trial was tomorrow. There was still so much left to do.

She'd already interviewed the five witnesses who were going to testify—Paul, Ryan, Kevin, Malik, and Jack—to find out exactly what they remembered about the day of the crime when they were at Jack's house. She'd written out index cards for David Kirkorian that told him exactly what he was supposed to say during the trial.

WHEN THE TRIAL BEGINS:

You bang your gavel and say:
"All rise! Court is in session.
The Honorable David P.
Kirkorian presiding."

IF SOMEBODY TALKS WHO'S
NOT SUPPOSED TO:

You say: "Order in the court!
Order in the court! If you're not
quiet, I will hold you in
contempt!"

WHEN YOU SWEAR IN A WITNESS:

You say: "Do you swear to
tell the truth, the whole truth,
and nothing but the truth?"

Now she was finishing up coloring the map that showed where each person would stand or sit during the trial. And she still had to write her closing argument!

Jessie felt—for the first time in her life—as if she was about to take a test and she hadn't studied long enough.

"Let's just work a little longer," she said. "Are you almost done with the nametags?"

Megan showed Jessie the twelve jury nametags,

the five witness nametags,

and the judge's nametag.

63

"Those are good," said Jessie. "Now you just have to do the ones for the audience."

Megan groaned. "This is why Evan calls you Obsessie Jessie."

Jessie hated that nickname. She hated all nicknames! Why had Evan told Megan about that?

"I am not obsessed. I just work hard. It's called *due*"—she thought for a minute, but couldn't come up with the name—"something." She scrounged under the papers that were scattered on the floor and found "Trial by Jury," the booklet her mother had written. She started flipping through the pages.

"But we've been doing this for hours!" wailed Megan. "I want to go outside."

"Due diligence!" said Jessie. "That's what it's called. Doing your job so that later, no one can blame you and say you didn't work hard enough."

"Well, due diligence is BORING!" said Megan. She picked up the ruler that Jessie had been using to draw straight lines on her map and began to balance it upright in the palm of her hand. She was pretty good at it. Jessie was impressed.

Suddenly, Megan asked, "Do you think you can really prove that Scott stole Evan's money?"

Jessie felt her throat close up for an instant.

That was the question she was most afraid of. That was the question that had kept running through her mind last night as she lay in bed, trying to fall asleep.

"I don't know. I'd better be able to." Jessie imagined standing up in front of the whole class and apologizing to Scott. It made her feel like throwing up.

Megan put the ruler down and flopped onto the floor, spreading her arms and legs out like a starfish. She picked up the map Jessie had drawn that showed where everyone would be in the courtroom.

The courtroom wasn't a "room" at all. It was the grassy part of the school playground—the part that was farthest away from the building and the black-top and was shaded by a row of large elm trees. Jessie had drawn exactly where they would set up the milk crates and the jump ropes and the balls and who would sit where. Everybody's name was marked with some kind of symbol.

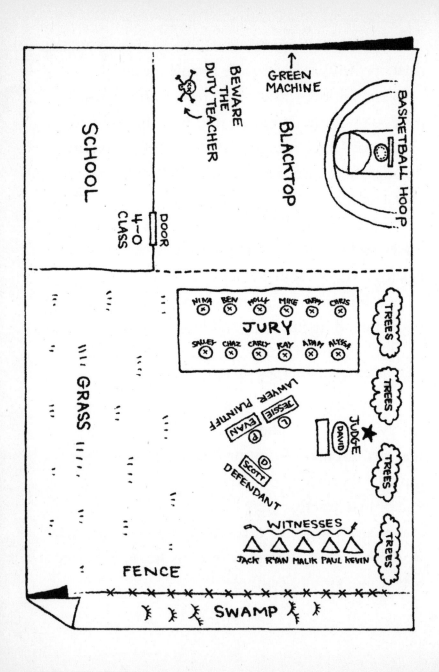

Megan stared at the map. "It's like I can almost imagine the whole thing happening," she said. "There's just one thing." She turned the paper one way, then the other. "It's not symmetrical. See?"

Jessie looked at the map. What was Megan talking about?

"It's supposed to be balanced, right? Everything even. But look." Megan pulled the pencil out of her ponytail and drew a light, dotted line down the middle of Jessie's drawing.

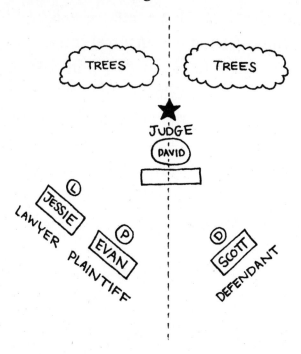

"Scott doesn't have a lawyer," she said. "The sides aren't even, so it's really not, you know, *fair*. I mean, to Scott."

"Well, it's his own fault," said Jessie. She'd worked too hard on her map to hear any criticism of it.

"But still," said Megan. "Isn't it the law that everyone gets to have a lawyer if they get arrested? Even if you're poor and even if no one likes you. And even if everyone thinks you're guilty. You get to have a lawyer. That's how they always do it on TV."

Jessie shrugged. "He wants to defend himself. You're allowed to do that in a real court."

Megan shook her head. "He only said that because there was no one left to pick. I mean, no boys." She looked at the map again. "It just doesn't seem right."

"What are you saying?" Jessie wished people would just be clear about what they meant. "Are you saying I'm wrong?"

Megan crossed her arms. "All I'm saying is that it isn't fair if Evan has a lawyer and Scott doesn't. And you know it, Jessie. You know it better than anyone else. You're—the Queen of Fair."

Another nickname! Was it an insult? The way Megan said "the Queen of Fair" didn't sound like an insult. But Jessie wasn't sure. Sometimes someone said something one way and meant it exactly the opposite. That was called *sarcasm*, and Jessie always missed it, like a pitch thrown too fast, leaving her swinging at nothing but air.

Outside, Jessie could hear the steady bouncing of a basketball in the driveway. Evan. Shooting hoops. Did he even know how hard she was working—for *him?*

Then the bouncing stopped, and she heard a car pull into the driveway. Megan heard it, too. "That's my mom," she said. "Gotta go." Megan had a dentist appointment at four o'clock.

For the first time ever, Jessie was glad to see Megan go.

Chapter 8
Defense

defense (dǐ-fěns'), *n.* The argument presented in a court of law to prove the innocence of the accused; (in sports) the act of protecting your goal against the opposing team.

It wasn't hot enough to sweat, but Evan was sweating. Two wide rivers ran down the sides of his face, and every time he spun he could feel droplets flying off the tips of his hair.

He was going to get this shot right even if it killed him.

He'd been working on it all afternoon. Actually, he'd been working on it all month. It was a turn-around jumper from the top of the key. A good fifteen feet from the basket, and he was shooting with his left hand. That's what all the greats could do—shoot with their weak hand and still make the basket. Evan's dad used to say to him: "Work from your weak side, and no one will be able to defend against you."

Evan turned his back to the basket and planted his feet on the painted lines of the driveway. He dribbled once, dribbled twice, dribbled three times, then—like a rocket shooting off its launching pad, he sprang into the air and pivoted his whole body around. Even as his body was falling back to the ground, he got off the shot, falling away from the basket as the ball sailed toward the pole and—

missed.

Sometimes he made it; sometimes he didn't. About one time out of every ten he made the shot. Evan wanted to flip that around so that only one time out of every ten he *missed*. It was a killer shot. If he had that kind of shot in his pocket, he could beat anyone on the court.

Dribble once, dribble twice, dribble three times . . .

"Hey, Evan."

Evan straightened up and looked toward the street. Megan was riding her bike toward him. She came to a sliding stop, then hopped off her bike before walking it across. Evan shook to get some of the sweat out of his eyes. Then he ducked his head and wiped his face on the sleeve of his T-shirt. Girls do not like sweat.

"I thought you had a dentist appointment," he said as she pushed her bike onto the driveway.

"It was short. Just a checkup," she said. "Is Jessie still in there?" Megan nodded her head in the direction of the house.

"Yeah. Still getting ready for The Big Day." Evan was dreading the trial. Every fourth-grader was going to be there—on the playground after school tomorrow—and what if Jessie couldn't prove that Scott Spencer was guilty? She wasn't a real lawyer. And could Evan really count on his friends? It seemed like every day this week Paul and Ryan had gone to Scott's house after school. Maybe by the time of the trial, all the guys would be on

Scott's side. Evan imagined standing up in front of the whole class and apologizing to Scott. He dribbled the ball, as if he could drum that idea out of his head.

"Wow," said Megan. "She gets kind of like . . ."

"Obsessed," said Evan. Then again, he thought about what *he'd* been doing all afternoon. How many times had he practiced that shot? One hundred? Two hundred? And he planned to keep going until it got too dark to see the basket. So maybe it ran in the family.

As if she was reading his thoughts, Megan asked, "You been out here the whole time?"

"I'm working on a shot. You want to see?"

Megan shrugged and smiled, and Evan decided that meant yes. He set his feet and started his dribbling rhythm. *Please let it fall, please let it fall, please let it fall,* he said in his head as he bounced the ball on the blacktop.

But it didn't. It *ka-thunked* off the backboard and ricocheted toward the street. Evan had to run fast to save it from rolling into the road.

"That was close," said Megan. "You're really good."

Evan shook his head as he dribbled the ball back to the center of the paint. "Close doesn't count in basketball. You either make the shot or you don't."

"Well, it was better than I could have done," she said. "And I'm the best shooter on my team."

Evan raised his eyebrows. "You play basketball?"

"And soccer," she said. "But I'm better at basketball."

"Really? Can you make a three-pointer?"

Megan laughed. "Sometimes."

"So, let's see," said Evan. He tossed the ball to her, and she dribbled across the driveway so that her feet were just outside the three-point line.

Evan watched as Megan handled the ball, watched the way her ponytail bounced back and forth and her bracelets danced up and down her arm.

"Okay, here goes," she said. "Don't hold your breath, though." She lifted the ball over her head, then sent it sailing through the air like water shooting out of a garden hose. It landed right in the basket.

"Awesome!" said Evan. He scooped up the bouncing ball and made an easy lay-up. "You want to shoot some? We could play HORSE. Or one-on-one, if . . . " Evan thought about defending against a girl, and his stomach turned over on itself. How did you defend against someone without ever touching them?

"Can't," said Megan, looking down the road. "I'm going over to someone's house."

"Whose?" asked Evan, bouncing the ball back and forth between his legs. He was a pretty good shooter, but he was a great ball handler. When he made it to the pros, he'd probably be a point guard. Sure, they didn't get all the glory, but point guards ruled the court.

Megan waved her hand up the street, but didn't say a name as she strapped on her bike helmet.

Evan stopped dribbling. "Whose house?"

Megan kicked the pedal on her bike so that it spun backwards, the gears making a whirring sound like insects on a summer night. "Scott's. He said I could try out his 20/20."

An elbow to the face, that's how her words felt. Evan squeezed the ball between his hands. "Are you like, *best friends* now?"

Megan gave him a look. "You don't have to be best friends to go to someone's house."

"Yeah, well, it sure looks like everyone is suddenly Scott's best friend." It seemed as if the 20/20 was all anyone talked about anymore. Scott was always the center of attention. And now. Now Megan was going over there, too. Evan scooped up the basketball and threw it hard against the garage door. It made a loud, angry, rattling sound as it hit. He threw it again. "All any of you care about is that stupid 20/20." Suddenly Evan realized that Scott didn't need a lawyer. He already had the best defense in town: the 20/20. Nobody would say Scott was guilty if it meant losing the chance to play with the coolest game system ever invented.

"Oh, c'mon," said Megan. "I bet you're dying to try it out, too."

Evan didn't respond. He just kept banging the ball against the garage door.

Megan pushed off on her bike and called out, "See you in school."

When she was halfway down the street, Evan shouted after her, "See you in *court!*"

Chapter 9
Bona Fide

bona fide (bō′nə fīd), *adj*. From the Latin, meaning "good faith," genuine, signifying "the real thing."

Jessie was hanging upside down on the Green Machine, her knees hooked over a monkey bar. This, she decided, was going to be the best Friday ever. After school, everyone would gather on the playground for the trial—even Megan, who had talked her mother into leaving later for their trip. Mrs. Overton had already given them permission to use the playground equipment after school. Jessie had her map. She had her note cards. She had practiced her closing argument at least twenty times. Evan had even listened to her practice and had given her some good tips on how to make the speech better. *Today is going to be great,* she thought.

At that moment, Scott Spencer walked over and stuck his face right next to hers.

"My *mom's* going to be my lawyer," he said.

"What?" said Jessie. She grabbed hold of the bar and flipped herself onto the ground. Everybody knew that Scott's mom was a big-time lawyer who worked downtown. Jessie had heard a million times about how fancy her office was. Scott said you could see the whole city from her office window. Sometimes her name was even in the newspaper.

"That's right. My mom. She's going to mop up the floor with you. She's going to bury you alive!"

Jessie squinted her eyes at Scott. "She's taking a day off from work?"

"No," said Scott, sneering at Jessie. "But she said she'd leave early. I told her it was important, and she said she'd be here."

"Well—she—can't," said Jessie, stammering. "It's for kids only. No grownups allowed."

"Are you saying I can't have a lawyer?"

"I didn't say that," said Jessie. But she was stuck, and she knew it. Everybody has the right to legal counsel. It was on page two of "Trial by Jury." It was the law. "Fine," she said, pressing her lips together. "But she'd better not be late."

Jessie remembered those words that afternoon as she ran around the playground, madly trying to set up the courtroom so the trial could start on time.

Thank goodness Mrs. Overton had let them use the playground equipment without asking any questions. She had made it clear that it was Evan's responsibility to bring everything back when they were done playing. Even though it was Friday afternoon and school was over for the day, he was still technically the Equipment Manager until Monday morning.

By quarter to three, Jessie had carried all the equipment outside and set up the milk crate under the elm trees, standing it up on end so that it looked like a podium. On top of the crate she placed the pile of index cards that told David Kirkorian *exactly* what he was supposed to say, then she called David over. He was holding a real wooden gavel in one hand and a brown paper bag in the other.

"Look what I borrowed from my dad," said David, waving the gavel. "It was a gag gift, and he said we could use it."

"What's in there?" asked Jessie, pointing to the bag.

David reached into the bag and pulled out a bunched-up ball of black cloth. He slipped it over his head. The cloth puddled at his feet. "It's my brother's graduation robe," he said. "I know it looks big, but just wait." He stepped behind the podium so that the milk crate covered all the extra fabric dragging on the ground. Jessie had to admit, it made him look like a real judge. And when he banged the gavel on a block of wood he'd brought, Jessie felt maybe she really could count on David Kirkorian to do his part.

In front of the milk crate, Jessie placed two basketballs, one for Evan to sit on and one for Scott. Jessie's "chair" was the dodge ball, and she set it up right next to Evan's. Should she set up the other dodge ball for Scott's mother to sit on? She couldn't imagine a grownup sitting on a ball the way kids did, so she left the second dodge ball in the crate. Off to one side, she stretched out the jump ropes to form a box on the grass where the jurors would sit, and on the other side she put down a squiggly jump rope that marked where the witnesses would stand while they waited to testify. There were only six people in the audience, so Jessie figured that they could just sit behind the three Frisbees that she had carefully placed on the grass.

"It looks great!" said Megan, walking over to Jessie.

Jessie looked around. For the first time, she could actually *see* the courtroom. It wasn't just a picture in her head. It wasn't just a map drawn on a piece of paper. It was a bona fide court. The real deal.

She nodded, a single butterfly tickling the inside of her stomach. "So far, so good."

Chapter 10
Trial by Jury

trial by jury (trī′əl bī jŏŏr′ē), *n.* A legal proceeding in which the guilt or innocence of a person accused of a crime is decided by a group of his or her peers, rather than by a judge or panel of judges.

Evan looked around and felt as though he'd dropped into an alternate universe.

First of all, he was sitting on a basketball, which felt strange.

Second, here was his sister, acting like she was the leader of the free world. Jessie could sometimes be bossy at home, but Evan was used to seeing her on the sidelines at school. On the edge of whatever was happening on the playground. Eating quietly at a cafeteria table. Sitting with her hands in her lap at the all-school assemblies.

Suddenly she was the leader. And it was weird.

Evan stared at the twelve kids sitting in the jury box, and that was weird, too. If he looked at each kid, one at a time, all he saw were the faces of kids he'd known for most of his life. Nothing new. But when he looked at them all together, standing in the box that Jessie had made out of jump ropes, they looked different. Even Adam, his best friend in the world, seemed almost unfamiliar. They were the jury—the ones who would either hand him a new Xbox 20/20 or make him stand up in class and apologize in front of everybody. Suddenly, they didn't seem like the kids he'd known forever. They had turned into something much bigger.

Evan's eyes traveled across the courtroom: to the witnesses all standing together behind the line of the jump rope, to the audience waiting patiently for the trial to begin, and to David Kirkorian standing at his milk-crate podium.

And that was the weirdest thing of all. Every single one of the fourth-graders had shown up after school and put on a nametag. (Okay, so Malik had taped his nametag to his butt, but he was still standing in the witness box, ready to testify.) Everyone was waiting to do whatever Jessie told them to do. It was as if all of a sudden there was a whole new set of rules at school, and everyone—*everyone*—had agreed to follow them.

Even Scott Spencer was sitting on his basketball. He had his knees spread wide, and he was drumming a beat on the ball. *Chook-uh-ta-chook, chook-uh-ta-chook, chook-uh-ta-chook.* He had that look. That Scott Spencer look. The look in his eyes that seemed to say, *It's all good. It's all cool. It's all mine.*

That was the thing about Scott Spencer. Somehow, some way, he always managed to spin things so that everything worked to his advantage. Evan remembered the time they were in first grade, playing in Scott's basement playroom. Scott's mom was at work. His dad worked at home, like Evan's mom did, but his office was all the way at the other end of the house, and it was soundproof! Evan remembered how they used to play a game of seeing who could make enough noise to get Mr. Spencer to come out of his office. They practically had to set off a bomb to get him to come out!

So that day, they were playing pick-up sticks for pennies, betting a penny on every game. At first Scott was winning, and Evan had lost about seven cents. But then Evan started catching up, and then he was ahead, and Scott owed him eleven whole cents, which seemed like a lot of money back then. "Hey, let's get a snack," said Scott, and they could have gone all on their own to get something out of the kitchen, but instead Scott went to his dad's office and asked him to bring them something in the playroom. And of course when Scott's dad saw that they were betting pennies, he ended the game and made Evan return everything he'd won. "Betting isn't allowed in this house," he'd said. But Evan had thought to himself, *Losing, that's what's not allowed.*

Evan looked at Scott. Evan wasn't a fighting kid.

He'd only gotten in two fistfights in his whole life, and one of them had been with Adam, his best friend! Both those fights had been fast and furious, and then they'd been over. No hard feelings. Apologies all around. Everyone agreeing not to fight anymore.

Why couldn't it be that way with Scott? What was it about him that made Evan's blood boil? That turned one thing into another—a fight about some missing money into a full-blown trial by jury? Evan opened his mouth to say something to Scott—

Which is exactly when David K. picked up the gavel, banged it on the block of wood, and read from the top index card, "All rise! Court is in session. The Honorable David P. Kirkorian presiding."

Chapter 11
Perjury

perjury (pûr′jə-rē), *n.* Purposely telling a lie in a court of law after taking an oath to tell the truth and only the truth.

"Will the lawyer for the prosecution please step forward?" said Judge Kirkorian. The defense lawyer, Scott's mother, still hadn't arrived, but they couldn't wait any longer. About half the jury had to be home by four o'clock.

Jessie stood up and addressed the court. She made her voice sound strong. "Ladies and gentlemen of the jury, for my first witness, I call Jack Bagdasarian."

Jack walked up to the podium, and David told

him to put his right hand over his heart and raise his left hand in the air.

"Do you swear to tell the truth, the whole truth, and nothing but the truth?" asked David.

"I do," said Jack, standing straight as a pole.

"You may proceed," said David, turning to Jessie.

Jessie walked up to Jack. "Mr. Bagdasarian," she said. "Where were you on the day of Sunday, September fifth?"

"What do you mean?" asked Jack. "Is that the day Scott stole the money?"

"Hey! I didn't steal the money!" yelled Scott.

"Says you!" shouted Malik, and everybody began yelling.

"Call for order," Jessie hissed at David, who was just standing there, watching it all, like it was a movie on television.

David shuffled through his index cards until he found the right one. Then he banged the wooden gavel on the block of wood. "Order in the court! Order in the court! If you're not quiet, I will hold you in"—he looked more closely at his card—"contempt!" David waved the card and added, "That means you'll get sent home. And when you come to school on Monday, we won't tell you what happened, either."

Everybody got really quiet then.

Jessie turned to her witness again. "September fifth was the day everyone went to your house to swim," she said. "Can you tell the court what you remember about that day?"

So Jack told the story: They'd all been playing basketball on the playground—Evan and Jack and Paul and Ryan and Kevin and Malik—but it was really hot, and they decided they wanted to swim at Jack's house. So Jack had gone home to ask his mom if it was okay, and when he came back to the playground, Scott was there, too, so then they'd all gone back to Jack's house.

"And then what happened?" asked Jessie, pacing back and forth in front of the podium. She was holding a pencil and carrying her Writer's Notebook tucked under her arm. It made her feel more official.

"We played pool basketball," said Jack. "I've got one of those floating hoops, so we just goofed around and stuff."

"Did Evan swim in his own bathing suit or did he borrow one from you?" asked Jessie.

"I think he borrowed one," said Jack. "Yeah, I'm pretty sure he did. And so did Scott."

"So both Evan and Scott changed into borrowed bathing suits at your house. Is that correct?"

"Yep," said Jack, bobbing his head up and down.

"And where did they put their regular clothes when they went swimming?" asked Jessie, pointing her finger at Jack so that the jury would know she was getting to the good part.

"In my room, I guess. That's where everyone puts their shoes and socks and stuff at my house, 'cause if you leave anything downstairs, the dog gets it."

"So let me be clear on this point," said Jessie, standing directly in front of Jack. "Evan's shorts— and whatever was in his pockets—were in *your* room. And Scott's shorts—and whatever was in his pockets—were also in your room. Is that correct?"

"Yeah. I already said that."

Jessie turned to the jury. "I just want to make sure that everyone knows that fact. Evan's and Scott's shorts were in the same room." She turned back to Jack. "One more question for you, Mr. Bagdasarian. Did anyone get out of the pool and go inside?"

"Well, sure," said Jack, laughing. "I mean, jeez, we were drinking like ten gallons of lemonade and eating watermelon slices. You can't hold *that* in forever."

The courtroom burst into laughter, but David banged his gavel so loudly that everyone quieted right down. Nobody wanted to get sent home before there was a verdict.

"Did *Scott* go into the house?" asked Jessie.

"Uh-huh," said Jack.

"Did he go in *alone?*"

"Yeah."

"And how long was he in the house *alone?*"

"I don't know," said Jack, shrugging.

"Long enough to run upstairs and steal an envelope filled with money out of Evan's shorts?" asked Jessie.

"Sure," said Jack. "He was in there for a while. And I know he went into my room, because he came down dressed."

"Dressed?" asked Jessie. "Why did he do that?"

"He said he had to go, right away."

"But did he say why?"

"No. Just said he had to go."

"Did he leave in a hurry?"

"You should have seen him. He went tearing out of there. I don't think he even had both shoes on when he left."

"I don't suppose you happened to check his pockets before he left, did you?"

"Uh, no," said Jack.

"Too bad," muttered Evan. Jessie looked over at her brother. He didn't look happy.

"That will be all," said Jessie.

"The witness is excused," said David in his serious judge voice, and when Jack didn't move, he added, "You may step down."

"Step down?" asked Jack, looking at the ground.

"You may go back to the witness area," said David, and he gave Jack a look that made Jack close his mouth and do what he was told.

Jessie called up the witnesses one by one, and each boy said the same thing: Scott had gone into the house to use the bathroom, came out a while later dressed, and then rushed out the door. Hearing the story five times made it seem like it was the absolute truth.

Jessie was feeling good. So good, she decided to call Evan to the stand. She hadn't planned out any questions to ask him, but that didn't matter. Everyone liked Evan, and Jessie knew it was a good strategy to put a likable witness on the stand.

But when she said, "For my next witness, I call Evan Treski to the stand," Evan shot her a furious look. He walked up to the judge's podium like he was walking to the gallows. When he turned to face the court, he had both thumbs hooked in his back pockets, and his shoulders were hunched forward. What was wrong? thought Jessie. They were going to win!

"Mr. Treski," Jessie began. "Can you please tell the court where you were on the afternoon of September fifth?"

"We already know that!" shouted Taffy Morgan, who was sitting in the second row of the jury box. "Ask him something *different!*"

"Yeah!" shouted Tessa James from the audience. "Ask him where he got all that money from. That's what I want to know."

Ben Lesser shouted out the same thing: "Ask him that!" And Nina Lee echoed, "Yeah, ask him that!"

Slowly, Jessie felt her face turning hot. That was the *last* question she wanted to ask Evan while he was on the stand. If the jury found out that Evan had stolen that money from her—it would be all over. Some of the kids in the jury box started to chant, "Ask him! Ask him!"

"Order in the court!" shouted David. When everyone quieted down, he said to Jessie, "That's a good question. Why don't you ask him that?"

"He's *my* witness," said Jessie, "and I get to make up the questions." Jessie knew the rules: She was the lawyer, and nobody could make her ask her witness a question she didn't want to ask. "I'll ask what I want, and I don't want to ask that."

"What?" said Scott. "Have you got something to hide?"

"Leave her alone," said Evan.

"Yeah, leave me alone," said Jessie, looking from David to Scott to Evan.

"Fine," said Scott, crossing his arms and looking smug. "Don't ask him. I'll just have my mom ask him where he got the money."

"Your mom's not even here," said Jessie angrily. "And I bet she won't show up, either."

Scott jumped up to his feet and looked like he was going to take a swing at Jessie. "She will, too. She's just late, that's all. 'Cause she's a *real* lawyer, with *real* work to do. Not like you! You faker!"

"Order in this court, or I will throw you both out!" shouted David. He even stepped in front of the podium and swung his gavel over his head like he was going to bean someone with it. Then he turned to Jessie and said, "You might as well ask

Evan the question, Jessie. He's going to end up answering it anyway."

And Jessie knew he was right.

She'd really made a mess of this. And she'd been feeling so good. So confident. So sure of herself.

"Mr. Treski," she said, "where did you get the money—the two hundred and eight dollars—that you had in your pocket on that day?"

You could have heard a pin drop—except that a pin wouldn't have made any noise at all because of the grass. But it was *quiet* in the court. Even the birds seemed to fall silent as if they were waiting to hear the answer.

Evan mumbled something, and Jessie had to ask him to repeat what he said.

"I took it from your lock box," said Evan, looking at her like he wanted to squash her like a bug.

Nobody said a word. Everyone stared at Evan, and Evan stared at Jessie.

"You *stole* it?" asked Paul, his eyes wide with surprise.

"Man, you never told us *that* part of the story," said Adam, shaking his head.

"Wow. You stole money from your little sister?" said Scott, smiling for the first time all afternoon. "That is *low*."

Jessie looked down at the ground. She knew that Evan was staring at her with a look that said, *I wish you'd never been born.*

"Excuse me?" said a voice from the audience. Jessie turned. It was Megan, and she was raising her hand, like she was in class.

"The bench recognizes Megan Moriarty," said David.

"The bench can't recognize someone from the audience," said Jessie. "The audience isn't allowed to talk during a trial. This is all wrong."

"Well," said David. "I'm the judge, so I get to decide. Megan!"

"Was that my money, too?" Megan asked. She looked straight at Evan. "Was half of that two hundred and eight dollars mine from the lemonade stand?"

Jessie's mouth fell open, but no sound came out. Evan dropped his head into his hands.

Things were coming out in this trial that Jessie had never expected to come out. Like the fact that

Evan had stolen the money from Jessie before Scott stole the money from Evan. Or the fact that half the money he'd lost had been Megan's money. And just because Evan had planned to return the money to Jessie a day later—and she'd forgiven him for taking it in the first place—and just because Jessie and Evan had worked really hard to earn back all of Megan's money so that she'd *never know* she lost it—those facts didn't seem to matter much at all. In the eyes of everyone, it looked like Evan was a thief. A lying thief.

All of a sudden, words started to fly out of Jessie's mouth. "He didn't steal it," she said. "*I* told him to take the money. I gave it to him for safekeeping. He *didn't* steal it." Jessie turned to Megan. "It's my fault your money got stolen."

Evan looked at her. Megan looked at her. Scott looked at her. Everyone in the courtroom stared at Jessie. And all Jessie could think was that she had just told a lie in court. And everyone knew it.

Chapter 12
Sixth
Amendment

Sixth Amendment (sĭksth ə-mĕnd′mənt), *n.* The part of the U.S. Constitution that explains the rights of anyone who is accused of a crime and brought to trial, including the right to legal counsel.

Jessie whispered, "The prosecution rests," and she and Evan went back to their seats. Evan kept his eyes nailed to the ground. He didn't trust himself to look at Jessie. If he did, he knew that all his anger was going to spill over like lava pouring out of a crack in the earth's crust. He'd been humiliated—in front of the entire fourth grade. And even though he knew that Jessie hadn't done it on purpose, it was still *all her fault.* If she hadn't called him as a witness. If she hadn't made David the judge. If she hadn't given Scott Spencer that stupid arrest warrant in the first place, none of this would have happened.

David banged his gavel three times. "Will the lawyer for the defense please step forward?"

Evan saw Scott twist his head around and look at the parking lot. "We gotta wait a couple more minutes," said Scott, matter-of-factly. "My mom's not here yet."

"If she doesn't come," said Paul, "does Scott have to forfeit?"

David flipped through his cards. "Jessie? Does Scott forfeit if his mom doesn't come?"

"Here she is!" shouted Scott, jumping up from his ball. "I told you! I told you!" He turned to Jessie. "Now you're going to see how it's done by a *real* lawyer. She's going to make you look like a fool!" Scott ran off to the parking lot, where a large gray SUV was pulling up to the curb.

Evan watched as Scott ran up to the car and leaned in at the open window, talking with his mom. Scott turned around and pointed at all the kids, sitting in the courtroom. Evan could just barely see Mrs. Spencer, her hands on the wheel, the engine of the car still running. Then Scott stepped back from the car, and it drove away.

Scott came walking back and sat down on his basketball. He shrugged, but Evan could tell it was an act. "She can't stay," said Scott. "She's got a big meeting. Real stuff, not kids' stuff." He shrugged again and looked straight ahead at David, avoiding everyone else's eyes.

"So . . . ?" said David. "What do we do now?" Everyone in the courtroom turned to Jessie, who had been keeping quiet ever since she sat down.

Evan looked at Jessie. She wasn't smiling, and that surprised him. After all, this meant they won, right? At least, that's how it worked in basketball. If the other team didn't show up or didn't have enough players, then they forfeited the game, and that meant your team won automatically. Usually, Evan hated forfeit games, even if it meant winning. He'd rather play and lose than win by forfeit. But this time, Evan would take a win any way he could get it. The image that had been haunting him for days—of standing up at Morning Meeting and apologizing to Scott—began to fade, and a new one took its place: Evan playing with his new Xbox 20/20—with all his friends over at *his* house.

Jessie said, "David, you say, 'Will the lawyer for the defense please step forward,' and then Scott says—well, whatever he wants to say in his own defense, and then he says, 'The defense rests,' and that's it."

"And then the verdict!" said Salley Knight, who was in the jury box. "Then we vote and give the verdict!"

"Right," said Jessie, glumly.

What was her problem? wondered Evan. They were sure to win if Scott had no defense lawyer.

"Ahem." David cleared his voice. "Will the lawyer for the defense please step forward?"

Everyone turned to look at Scott, but it was a

voice from the back of the courtroom that broke the silence.

"That would be me." Megan stood up from the audience and walked to the front of the courtroom.

What?

At first Evan thought he must have heard wrong.

Did Megan Moriarty just say that she was going to defend Scott Spencer?

"You can't do that," said Evan, jumping up from his seat. "You're . . . you're . . ." He wanted to shout, *You're supposed to be on my side, not his!,* but he couldn't say that. Not in front of the whole fourth grade.

"Hey!" shouted David, banging his gavel once. "Order in the court. Plaintiff, sit down. If you keep making a disturbance, I'll have you thrown out of court!"

"Oh, right! Like you could!" said Evan, but he sat down on his basketball anyway.

"Jessie," said David, holding up his watch. "It's three-thirty. I've got to go in ten minutes. Is this allowed?"

Jessie nodded her head. "Yes. It's . . . fair."

Evan couldn't believe it. Was this really happening? Was the girl he was *in love with* about to destroy his one and only chance for revenge against his sworn enemy?

Megan turned to Scott. "Do you still not want a girl lawyer?"

Once again, Scott shrugged. "You're all I got. I guess it's okay."

"All right," said Megan. "This won't take long. Can I call my first witness?"

David nodded, and Megan moved to the front of the courtroom.

Chapter 13
Circumstantial Evidence

circumstantial evidence (sûr′kəm-stăn′shəl ĕv′i-dəns), *n.* Indirect evidence that makes a person *seem* guilty. For example, if a suspect is seen running away from the scene of a crime, a jury might assume that he's guilty of the crime, even though no one saw him commit it.

Megan started with Jack. She asked him three simple questions and told him to answer with just one word: *yes* or *no.*

"Jack, did you ever see the money in Evan's shorts pocket?"

"No."

"Did you see Scott Spencer take anything out of Evan's pocket?"

"No."

"Since that day, have you ever seen Scott Spencer carrying around two hundred and eight dollars?"

"No."

Then, one by one, she called Kevin, Malik, Ryan, and Paul to the witness stand and asked the same three questions. Their answers were all the same—*no*.

Listening, Jessie felt miserable—but she was impressed. In less than five minutes, Megan had unraveled her whole case against Scott Spencer. The truth was, nobody had actually *seen* anything that day at the pool. It was all just guessing about what had happened to Evan's money.

The whole time Megan was asking the witnesses questions, Jessie worried that Megan was going to call Evan to the stand for cross-examining. She knew that Evan would rather pull his hair out, one strand at a time, than get back up on that witness stand. But instead Megan called a different witness—one that even Jessie didn't expect.

"My last witness," Megan said to the jury, "is Scott Spencer."

Scott Spencer had been slouching forward, sitting on his ball, his elbows resting on his knees, his eyes on the ground. Now he straightened up and squared his shoulders. He looked as surprised as anyone to hear his name called out in court.

"I don't want to," he said. He looked defiantly at Megan and then at David, as if he was going to challenge both of them to a fight.

David pointed his gavel at him. "Well, you have to. You've got to do what your lawyer says."

Jessie was fairly certain that this wasn't true. She thought she remembered a rule that said you didn't have to testify against yourself in court, but she wasn't positive, so she didn't say anything.

Scott stood up, shoving his basketball with his heel so that it rolled a few feet toward the back of the courtroom. He walked to the podium and put his right hand over his heart and raised his left.

"Do you swear to tell the truth, the whole truth, and nothing but the truth?" asked the judge.

"Yeah," said Scott, but he said it long and low, like the word was being pulled out of his mouth on a rope.

"I just have one question," said Megan, "and it's an easy one." She put her hands on her hips and faced him straight on. "Did you really pay for your new Xbox 20/20 with your own money?"

"What?" said Scott, like he couldn't believe what he'd just heard. He turned to David K. "I'm not going to answer that. I don't have to answer that question."

"Yes, you do!" said David. "Or I'll hold you in contempt." He banged his gavel sharply once to let Scott know that he was serious.

Jessie looked at Scott and knew exactly how he felt. *Everyone* was staring at him.

"Well—I—" Not a single person made a sound. Even the branches of the elm trees stopped moving, the gentle rustling of the leaves dying down to silence.

"Remember," said Megan quietly. "You're under oath."

Scott made a sour face. "*No.* I didn't. You happy?" He smirked at Megan. "My parents bought it for me."

Everybody started shouting then. "I knew it! I knew it!" said Adam. David had to whack his gavel about ten times to get 4-O to quiet down. "The witness is excused! Closing arguments! The prosecution goes first! Hurry up!"

Jessie stood up. This was supposed to have been her big moment.

"I wrote a really great closing argument," she said, pulling some index cards from her back pocket, "but I guess we don't have time for it. So I'll just say this."

She walked over to the jury box. Twelve pairs of eyes stared right back at her. Some of the jurors, like Adam and Salley, she knew well enough, but most of them she hardly knew at all. Now they were all looking at her. Everyone in the jury box was waiting to hear what she had to say.

"Ladies and gentlemen of the jury," she began.

"The facts are the facts. The money was in Evan's shorts, safely folded up in Jack's room. Scott went into Jack's room and then went running home, like a guilty crook. When Evan went upstairs, his shorts were unfolded and the money was gone. It doesn't take a genius to solve this crime. In the end, it comes down to who's telling the truth. So think of all the years you've known Evan Treski and all the years you've known Scott Spencer, and ask yourself this: Who do *you* believe?"

Jessie stuffed her index cards back in her pants pocket. She hadn't even gotten to use them. And she'd spent all that time writing a really great closing argument. This trial was nothing like what she'd thought it would be.

"Okay, done," said David. "Now, the closing argument for the defense. *Fast,* Megan."

Megan stood up and walked to the jury box. "Here's the thing," she said. "You can't convict Scott, because there's absolutely no proof. It's all just us imagining what happened. We don't know for sure, because nobody *saw* anything, and the money never turned up, so . . . we just don't know. And I guess we'll never really know what happened that afternoon." Megan looked at David. "That's it," she said.

"Done!" shouted David, banging his gavel again. "Jury, make your decision!"

"My mom's here!" said Salley Knight, noticing a car parked in the parking lot.

"So's mine," said Carly Brownell.

"Jury! Huddle up!" shouted Adam. All twelve members of the jury formed a tight circle, their heads bowed together, their backs to the courtroom.

Jessie stood up, then sat down, then stood up again. She felt that dangerously bubbly feeling she sometimes got in her stomach. She started to think: If she had to throw up, where would be the best place to do it? Behind the podium? By the trees? Could she make it to a bathroom in time? She wished she could talk to Evan, but one look at him told her she'd better stay clear. His mouth was clenched so tight, it looked like he would bite through his own teeth.

"Break!" shouted Adam, clapping his hands together loudly. The jury huddle broke up, and Jessie saw Adam quickly scribble something on a slip of paper, then hand the paper to David.

"All rise to hear the verdict of the jury," said David. Everyone stood.

Jessie felt her breath catch in her throat. She tried to swallow, but it was as if the muscles in her neck were paralyzed. A picture swam into her head: standing up in front of the whole class and apologizing to Scott Spencer.

"My mom's coming over," said Carly, pointing to the parking lot. Jessie turned to see a tall woman wearing sunglasses and a baseball cap heading toward them.

"Hurry up!" said Adam.

"Okay," said David, his voice rising to a squeak. "I'm supposed to say all this official stuff, but I'll just read the verdict out loud! The verdict is—not guilty!"

"Yes!" shouted Scott Spencer, jumping in the air and double-pumping both fists over his head. "I win! Man, I cannot wait for Monday morning!"

But nobody else moved. And nobody else said a word.

Something had gone terribly wrong out here on the playground. In the shade of the elm trees, away from the scolding eyes of duty teachers and parents, the kids in 4-O had created a court all their own and followed all the rules—but somehow come out with the wrong answer. Jessie felt it, and so did everyone else. Jessie was sure of it.

"Are we done?" asked David, holding his gavel aloft. "Jessie?"

Jessie nodded.

"This court is adjourned," David said, and hit the gavel once on the wooden block, just as Carly Brownell's mother came up alongside her daughter.

"What are you kids playing?" she asked.

"Nothing," said Carly. She picked up her book bag and headed for the parking lot with her mother. David stuffed the black robe and gavel into his brown paper bag and headed for the path. About half of the other kids followed, but the rest of the fourth-graders stayed where they were.

All of a sudden, a voice sliced through the air. "This is *not* over!"

Evan was standing with the basketball in his hands. "You and me!" he said, poking Scott Spencer in the chest so hard, Scott took a step back. "On the court. The basketball court."

Chapter 14
Fighting words

fighting words (fī′ting wûrdz), *n*. Words that are so venomous and full of malice that they cause another person to fight back physically. Fighting words are not protected as free speech under the First Amendment.

"You're on," said Scott.

Nobody bothered to pick up any of the equipment. The jump ropes, the Frisbees, the milk crate, the extra balls were all left right where they were. Instead, all the kids of 4-O who hadn't gone home lined up on either side of the basketball court.

Evan dribbled the ball, trying to get that feeling of looseness that helped him play his best. "We'll play to seven by ones. Straight up. King's court. And you have to take it past the big crack to clear." Evan pointed to the wide crack in the blacktop that ran twenty feet from the basket. That was the line they always used to clear the ball for half-court games.

"Who's the ref?" asked Scott.

"No ref, no fouls," said Evan. "Just play. If the ball falls through the hoop, it's a point. If it doesn't, go home and cry to your mother. Okay?" Evan was practicing his crossover dribbling while he talked. He was starting to feel his rhythm. He looked at Scott standing at the top of the key. There it was, that look on Scott's face—the one that seemed to say, *Why bother? I always win.* More than anything else, Evan wanted to wipe that look off Scott Spencer's face, once and for all.

"Yeah, okay," said Scott. "But who goes first?"

"You," said Evan, shooting him a chest pass so fast that Scott didn't even have time to put his arms up. The ball hit him in the chest and fell at his feet.

Evan heard some of the kids laugh and noticed Megan crossing her arms and frowning. "Good start!" shouted Paul from the sidelines, as Scott picked up the ball and cleared it behind the line.

"Nice, Treski," said Scott. "Real nice."

Evan ran up to the clear line and got low, ready to defend.

Scott dribbled the ball, hanging behind the line. Then he faked left and drove right, blowing past Evan.

Scott was quick, but Evan was quicker. He came up from behind, and just as Scott was shooting the ball, Evan clawed it out of the air, whacking it so hard it smacked down on the blacktop. On the way, his hand smashed into Scott's face. Scott crumpled to the ground. Undefended, Evan took the easy shot and scored his first point.

"You can't do that!" said Scott. "You *mauled* me!" He sat on the blacktop, his legs sprawled, looking like he couldn't even get up.

Evan rebounded and dribbled toward the clear line. He put a hand up to his ear and pretended to concentrate hard. "Do you hear a whistle, Scott? I guess not, 'cause there isn't one. *Man up.*"

Scott jumped to his feet, and Ryan yelled out, "Faker!"

"One–nothing," called out Adam. "Evan's ball."

Evan didn't even bother to juke. He just plowed right into Scott, driving him to the blacktop before charging the basket for the easy lay-up.

"Oh, man!" shouted Ryan.

Megan shook her head. "Why even call it basketball if you're going to play like that?"

Evan watched as Scott started to get up slowly. But he had already cleared the ball at the line and was charging to the basket before Scott got on his feet. He made another easy lay-up, as pretty as a bird.

"Three–zip," shouted Adam.

"Scott," said Ryan. "C'mon, show a little backbone."

This time, when Evan started his move to the basket, Scott lunged at the ball. He stripped it from Evan's hands, but the ball went shooting out of bounds.

"Out," shouted Adam. "Evan's ball!" So Evan took it out again, and this time he faked left, right, left, so that Scott was leaning the wrong way when Evan finally made his move.

"It's basketball, Scott. Not freeze tag!" called out Kevin.

Evan slowly dribbled the ball back. Scott faced him across the line, scowling, with his hands on his hips. "None of this counts," said Scott. "This is dirt ball. This is trash. None of this counts."

"Why not?" said Evan, dribbling steadily. "You agreed. No fouls. You said okay. Right?"

He took a step past the clear line, still dribbling the ball slowly right in front of his body. Then Evan spread his hands out wide, the ball bouncing between the two of them, unprotected. "Go on, take it!"

When Scott made his move, trying to grab the ball out of the air, Evan was ready. Faster than an eagle diving, he snatched the ball back, made a spin move around Scott, and drove for the basket. He jumped as high as he could, and just barely managed to stuff the ball with both hands through the hoop.

"Slammed!" screamed Paul, doing a dance on the sidelines.

"This is gross," said Megan. "I'm going home." She picked up her mailbag and slung it over her shoulder. "Jessie, are you coming?"

"No," said Jessie in a small voice. She was sitting on the grass, her knees pulled up to her chest. "I'll stay." Megan nodded, then walked toward the parking lot. Evan noticed her leaving, but told himself, *Who cares?*

"Four–nothing," said Adam. "Hey, Evan. Wrap it up, would you? I have to get home."

Evan quickly ran the score up to six–nothing with a jump shot from mid-key and a little floater right in front of the basket.

All the guys on the sideline were screaming *Shutout, shutout!,* and Evan dribbled the ball in time to their chant. He glanced at Scott. Scott was breathing so hard, he looked like he might throw up. Both his knees and one of his elbows were bloody. *He's right,* thought Evan. *This isn't basketball. It's revenge ball.*

"You want the ball?" asked Evan. "Here. You can have it." He let the ball roll off the tips of his fingers so that it dribbled over to Scott. "Don't say I didn't show you mercy," said Evan as Scott picked up the ball and they swapped places, Evan switching to defense. "Go on, I'll even back off. I'll give you all the room in the world. You still can't make a basket against me."

Scott dribbled the ball slowly, and Evan could see that he was trying to come up with a strategy. There was no way he could push past Evan, because Evan had the weight, and there was no way he could speed past him, because Evan was faster. The only way Scott Spencer was going to get the drop on Evan was by tricking him. That's all Scott had, thought Evan. That's all Scott ever had.

Scott started dribbling slowly toward the basket. Evan moved into position, blocking the lane, but still giving Scott plenty of room. He kept his eyes locked on Scott's.

Suddenly, Scott's mouth dropped open. He stopped dribbling the ball and shouted, "Oh, my god! Jessie, are you okay?"

Evan spun around. Where was she? Was she on the Green Machine? Had she fallen? She was such a klutz. She could hardly walk across a room without tripping.

Evan's eyes had just caught sight of her—Jessie, sitting on the sidelines, the way she always did, her knees tucked up to her chin, watching the game intently—when he figured it out. But by then Scott was past him, driving to the basket. Evan almost got there in time to block the shot, but almost doesn't count. Scott's shot was rushed and weak. It circled the rim—and then fell through.

"I can't believe you fell for that, dog!" shouted Kevin.

"The oldest trick in the book," said Paul, shaking his head.

"Six–one," shouted Adam. "Scott's ball."

Scott took the ball and shrugged as he dribbled past Evan. "King's court, right?"

Evan had never in his life had a feeling like this. Not when he broke his leg. Not when his father left. Not even when Jessie put bugs in his lemonade. This was worse. This was stronger. This felt like everything to him.

So when Scott made for the basket, Evan came at him with both hands up, and it must have been the look on his face that made Scott freeze and lose half a step. That's all it took. Evan stripped the ball and headed for the top of the key.

He could have just dribbled to the basket and made the shot, and that would have been that. The game would have been over. And he would have won.

But no.

He wanted to make Scott pay. He wanted to make sure that when they told the story—for days, for weeks, for years—of how Scott Spencer got *crushed* on the basketball court, they would talk about the final shot that Evan Treski made.

So he headed for the top of the key and planted his feet so that he could make that beautiful turn-around jumper that he'd been practicing for months. He stood there, dribbling the ball, practically shouting out to Scott, *Yeah, come get me.* And when Scott did, Evan turned and threw an elbow that caught Scott right on the side of the face.

Scott went flying and landed hard on his rear end, his hands scraping along the blacktop. Evan didn't even look over to see if Scott was okay. He dribbled once, twice, three times, then jumped in the air, twisted his body, and let fly the ball.

Everyone watched as it sailed through the air and then swooshed through the hoop.

Nothing but net.

The ball dropped to the blacktop and bounced. Nobody made a move for it. Nobody said anything. Scott was still sitting on the ground, the blood on his hands a bright red. Evan was standing, his arms at his side. He felt like he'd been through a fistfight.

Scott got up slowly, picked up the basketball, and then drop-kicked it as hard as he could so that it sailed over the fence and disappeared into the swamp. Then he ran.

Chapter 15
Balance

balance (băl′əns), _n._ A device used for weighing that has a pivoted horizontal beam from which hang two scales. In statues and paintings, the figure of Justice is often shown holding a balance.

"Grandma, can you talk for a minute?" Jessie stuck a moshi pillow behind her head and cradled the phone to her ear.

"Sure, Jessie Bean. What's up?" Jessie's grandmother lived four hours away, so Jessie called her on the phone a lot.

"Everything's awful," said Jessie, picking at a corner of her bedroom wallpaper that was peeling. She explained to her grandmother about the trial yesterday and the basketball game and Scott kicking the ball into the swamp. She told her how Evan had to hunt for the ball for half an hour before finally finding it, and how he told all his friends to just go home, he'd find it himself, *just go home*. So they did. And how Evan and Jessie were left to look for the ball, and how Evan didn't talk the whole time they did.

"And today he's not even *eating,* or anything," said Jessie. "Did you know that it's Yom Kippur?"

"Yom Kippur, is that the one where the kids dress up?" asked Jessie's grandmother.

"No, that's Purim." Grandma was always mixing up things like that, things that sounded kind of the same, but were different. During their last phone call, she was talking with Jessie about the sequoia trees in California, but she kept using the word *sequester* instead. "Yom Kippur is the day when the Jewish people ask for forgiveness and they don't eat."

"Is Evan Jewish now?" asked Grandma.

"No, but he's not eating. He says he's not hungry," said Jessie.

"Sometimes that happens to me," Grandma said. "I practically forget to eat."

"But Evan's *always* hungry," said Jessie. "Mom says he's a bottomless pit."

"He'll eat when he's ready," said Grandma. "Let it go."

Jessie hated it when her grandmother said that. She was always telling Jessie to *let it go* and *be the tree*. Crazy yoga grandma. How could anyone be a tree?

"But . . . I want to do something to help," said Jessie.

"Why don't you bake cookies?" said Grandma. "That'll get him to eat. Right?"

"I don't think so," said Jessie. "Not this time." This was bigger than cookies. How could she explain to her grandmother how bad things were?

Jessie had believed in the trial. She had thought the truth would come out in court, and with truth would come justice.

But instead of truth in the courtroom, there had been lies, including hers. Instead of justice, there was a crime with no punishment. And now she and Evan were going to have to stand up in front of the entire fourth grade and say that they had been wrong—even though Jessie knew that wasn't true.

"Grandma, it's so unfair," said Jessie. "I know Scott Spencer took that money. I know he's lying. And now it feels like I did all this work, just so he'd end up looking innocent!"

"Some things are beyond your control, Jessie," said her grandmother. "You need to learn to accept that. You can't run the whole world."

I wish I did, thought Jessie. The world would be a better place if she was in charge. But then . . . she thought of the terrible thing she'd done.

"Grandma," she blurted out. "I lied in court." She explained how it had happened. Her grandmother listened to the whole story without interrupting.

"Lying is wrong," Grandma said, "but at least you did it from a good place in your heart. You don't need to feel ashamed about loving your brother."

"I still feel really bad about it," said Jessie.

"That's good," said Grandma. "I'd be worried if

you didn't feel bad about lying. You *do* have control over that. Nobody can make you lie. So feel bad for a while, and always remember what you've learned, and then move on and be a better person. But don't beat yourself up, Jessie. You're only seven."

"Grandma! I'm eight!" said Jessie. How could her grandmother forget her age?

"Really?" said Grandma. "Are you sure?"

"I've been eight for almost a whole year. My birthday is next month."

"Good," said Grandma, "because I have a book I've been meaning to send you, and it will be the perfect birthday present."

"Grandma," said Jessie, her voice sounding a warning. "You're not going to send me *The Prince and the Pauper* again, are you?"

"No, Miss Smarty Pants! I remember I sent you that book—twice! You'll never let me forget that, will you?"

"Why do you forget things?" asked Jessie. "You didn't used to."

"Oh, Jessie Bean, I'm getting old." Her grandmother laughed quietly, and Jessie hugged the phone closer. "And that's something neither of us has any control over. Sorry to say."

Jessie heard the doorbell ring downstairs. She knew her mother wouldn't hear it all the way up in the attic office, and she was pretty sure that Evan wouldn't answer it, even if he did hear it. "Gotta go, Grandma," said Jessie. "There's someone at the door."

"Okay, Honey Bear. Be the tree! And bake cookies! I love you."

Jessie ran downstairs and opened the front door. There was Megan.

"Hi," said Megan.

Jessie lifted her hand in a short wave, but she didn't invite Megan in.

"I thought maybe you were mad at me," said Megan.

"Kind of," said Jessie. There was a short silence. "Why'd you do it?" Jessie hadn't wanted to believe that she was angry at her best friend, but now all the questions that she had tried to ignore since the trial came flooding into her brain. *Why'd you ruin all my hard work? Why'd you get Scott off the hook? Why'd you betray me and Evan?*

"I'm sorry, Jessie," said Megan. "I didn't want to make you mad, and I didn't want to mess up your trial, but the thing is, it wasn't really your trial. It was all of ours." Megan looked right at her. "You did this great thing, Jessie. You gave us a real court. Not some fake, dress-up, pretend thing. A real one. But in a real court of law, everyone has the right to a lawyer. So, somebody had to stand up for Scott. Otherwise, the trial would have been a great big fake."

Jessie didn't say anything, but she understood exactly what Megan was saying. Somewhere in the back of her brain, she'd known it all along. "I wanted to win," she said finally, feeling all over again the pain of losing. "But you're right. You did the right thing."

The two girls stood there, both looking at their feet. Why was it so hard to talk about feelings?

"I'm not mad at you anymore," Jessie said, knowing that it was mostly true and that by tomorrow it would be completely true.

Megan smiled. "See you on Monday, Jess." She hopped down the front steps.

"Hey, Megan?" called out Jessie. "Do you think Scott took the money?"

"Yep, I do," said Megan. She shrugged, and the look on her face seemed to say, *That's life.*

Jessie watched her friend walk down the street. It was a gorgeous end-of-summer-just-starting-to-be-fall day. The trees swayed in the breeze. The sky was the color of cornflowers. The sun felt good on her skin.

Jessie ran upstairs to her room and found the yoga book that her grandmother had given her the past Christmas. She flipped to page 48 and stared at the picture.

"Be the tree," Jessie murmured to herself. Slowly, she picked up her left foot and rested it on her right knee, finding and holding her balance for one blissful second.

Chapter 16
Amends

amends (ə-měndz′), *n.* Legal compensation (of money or other valuable assets) as a repair for loss, damage, or injury of any kind.

In his whole life, Evan had never gone this long without eating. And the weirdest thing of all was that he wasn't even hungry anymore. Sometime around two o'clock on Saturday afternoon, his hunger had just disappeared. Like turning off a light switch. He felt empty and light and a little buzzy in his head. But not hungry.

He hadn't even planned it. Yesterday, he'd come home and eaten his dinner, as usual. And then the sun went down and he thought about Adam and

Paul, and he wondered if they had started fasting and if they would make it all the way till tomorrow night. And then he wanted to see if he could do it. Go twenty-four hours without food. Just wanted to see what it was like, and if he had the strength to do it.

And that got him thinking about the Day of Atonement. The less he ate, the more he thought, until here he was, sitting on his branch of the Climbing Tree, way up high with the leaves whispering to him and the birds pecking for their last snack of the day and late-afternoon shadows beginning to stretch across the yard.

He began to think about his sins. And that was a hard thing to think about. Did he really have any sins? He didn't know. But there was one thing he did know. Right now, he felt lousy. And Evan knew that when he felt really bad, that usually meant he'd done something he regretted.

Evan regretted that whole basketball game. He wished he hadn't played like that. He wished Megan hadn't seen him play like that. Or Jessie. Or anyone. He wished he hadn't been such a jerk. The game kept playing over and over in his head, every perfect shot looping through his brain, and it made him feel sick. He was never going to know what had happened to that missing money, but crushing Scott on the basketball court wasn't going to change that.

Evan climbed down from the tree and went into the house. Jessie was in the kitchen with a mixing bowl and a bunch of ingredients spread out on the countertop: flour, sugar, butter, and eggs.

"What'cha makin'?" he asked as he walked through.

"Your favorite. Chocolate chip."

"Thanks," said Evan, grabbing his baseball hat from the front hall closet and heading for the door.

"Where are you going?" asked Jessie.

"Scott's."

"No!" said Jessie. "Don't do that."

"Quit worrying! Tell Mom where I went, okay?" Jessie followed him to the door. "And don't eat all the cookies before I get back," he shouted over his shoulder.

He didn't really have a plan. In the back of his

mind he figured a handshake and at least one "I'm sorry" were somewhere in his future. Beyond that, he didn't know what would happen.

Scott's house was a short bike ride away from Evan's, but his neighborhood was a world apart. The houses were huge and had fancy bushes planted in little groups and two-car attached garages and lawns that looked like they were edged with a razor blade. As Evan walked up the brick path to the front door, he noticed that the two large maple trees in the yard were beginning to turn. They would drop a lot of leaves next month, but Evan knew that Scott never had to rake because his family had a service that took care of the yard.

When the front door opened, Evan wasn't surprised to see Scott standing there. Evan could hardly ever remember Scott's parents answering the door.

He looked better than he had yesterday, that was for sure. Cleaned up, no blood, and he was wearing jeans, which covered up his knees. But the look on his face was the same—a look of hatred. Pure hatred beamed right at Evan.

"Hey," said Evan.

"What?" said Scott. "What do you want?"

Evan hadn't rehearsed what he was going to say, and now that he had Scott's angry face right in front of him, it was hard to come up with anything on the spot. He stood there for a minute, his mind a blank. What *had* he come here for?

And then he said the only thing he could think of. "I wanted to see your new 20/20."

That changed everything. Scott stopped scowling, and his arms loosened up. He waited just a second before saying, "Okay." Then he stepped back to let Evan through. That's how it had been, ever since they were little: Scott Spencer liked showing off his new toys.

Evan followed Scott down the flight of stairs to the finished basement, which was a combination playroom and family room. It was mostly the way that Evan remembered it: two couches, the computer desk, the file cabinet with the locked-up snacks, bins of toys and building things, sports equipment, the swinging chair that hung from the ceiling, an electronic keyboard, and a treadmill. The thing that caught his eye, though, was the new TV. It was enormous, the biggest flat-screen plasma that Evan had ever seen in his whole life.

"Wow!" said Evan.

Scott smiled. "Yeah, my dad bought that a few weeks ago. Cool, huh?"

Evan noticed the sleek white box hooked up to the TV. "Is that the 20/20?" he asked. "Wow, it's so small."

"Yeah, but watch what it can do."

Scott handed him two thick gloves that looked like hockey gloves, except that they were white, and a pair of heavy, dark goggles that wrapped all the way around his head. Evan took off his baseball cap and put the gloves and goggles on, then Scott pushed a button on the box. The next thing Evan knew, he was driving a car on a racetrack, with other cars whipping past him at about 120 miles per hour.

"Whoa!" shouted Evan.

"Turn to your right! With your gloves! Pretend you're holding a steering wheel and turn to your right!" screamed Scott.

Evan just barely missed crashing into the hay-stack barriers that protected the curves of the race-track. He quickly grabbed hold of an imaginary steering wheel and got himself back on the road.

"Squeeze your right hand to go faster, and your left hand to slow down," said Scott, turning up the volume so that the roar of the racecars filled Evan's ears. Evan could practically smell the exhaust fumes.

For the next five minutes, Evan took the ride of his life. He had never, ever played on a game system that was so much fun. No wonder Scott couldn't stop talking about it.

"Scott. Scott!" yelled a voice from behind.

Evan turned and whipped off the goggles. Mr. Spencer was standing at the top of the stairs. Scott jumped to turn down the volume on the TV.

"I've been calling you for the last five minutes. Will you turn that thing down? Do you have any idea how loud it is?"

"Sorry, Dad," said Scott. "We were just playing Road Rage."

"Well, you're going to blow out the speakers on the TV, and then *you'll* be the one to buy me a new one. And don't think I won't hold you to that. I didn't spend five thousand dollars on a new TV just so you could destroy it with your video games. That's an expensive piece of equipment, and you need to learn how to treat it with respect. Now keep it down. I'm trying to work."

"Yes, sir," said Scott.

Mr. Spencer turned and disappeared at the top of the stairs.

Scott picked up a baseball and started throwing it back and forth in his hands. Evan wasn't sure what to do. He put the gloves and goggles down on the floor. The racecars were still zooming by on the TV screen, but without any sound, they seemed silly and fake.

"Your dad works a lot, huh?" said Evan.

"Even on a Saturday," said Scott, throwing the ball.

"My mom works a lot, too," said Evan, but in his head he thought, *But at least she doesn't yell at us for making noise.*

"Yeah, whatever," said Scott. "You wanna play

Crisis? It's cool." And with that, he chucked the baseball to the corner of the room. Only it was harder than a chuck, and his aim was off. Way off. The ball winged across the room and caught the corner of the TV screen. There was a loud crash, and then the TV went dead.

Both boys froze. Evan couldn't make a sound. He felt like he had a sock stuffed down his throat. There was a foot-long crack in the TV screen and a bunch of smaller cracks that looked like a spider web. The house was completely silent except for the noise of Mr. Spencer's footsteps running down the stairs. And then he was there, standing in the door-way, staring at the TV.

"Did you do that on purpose?" he shouted at Scott.

"No!" said Scott. "I didn't . . ."

"Because you are going to pay for that. Every penny of it. Your allowance, your birthday money— forget Christmas presents this year. Do you understand?" A vein popped out on Mr. Spencer's forehead, like something in an alien movie. Every time he said a word that started with *p*—*pay, penny, presents*—white flecks of spit flew out of his mouth. Evan thought he was going to explode or something.

"Dad, I didn't . . ."

"That television is brand-new. *Brand-new*, do you hear me?"

Evan took half a sideways step toward Scott. "We're sorry. We didn't mean to do it. It was an accident."

Mr. Spencer looked at Evan for the first time since coming downstairs. It was almost like he'd forgotten there was anyone else in the room. Slowly, he breathed in and out. His teeth were clenched; his jaw was as hard as a rock wall. "Did *you* throw the ball?"

"No, but, we were, you know, playing, and the ball just kind of—hit the TV by mistake. We didn't do it on purpose." Evan was scared, but he couldn't help thinking what a jerk Mr. Spencer was. Sure, his mom got mad—plenty of times—and sometimes she yelled, but not when it was an honest accident.

"We're sorry, Dad," said Scott in a low voice.

"Well, that doesn't fix the TV, does it?" said Mr. Spencer. Without another word, he walked out.

The room was quiet.

"Okay, then," said Evan, just to fill the awkward silence.

Scott looked down at the ground. "Yeah," he said. He looked like his dog had just died.

Evan picked up his baseball cap and jammed it on his head, backwards. "So, this was fun," he said, deadpan, but Scott didn't smile, or even lift his eyes off the floor. Evan could understand. It was lousy when your own parent yelled like that in front of another kid. It made you feel like your whole family was just dirt. Scott probably wanted him to leave.

"Well, I'd better get home."

"Okay," said Scott. "And thanks. You know. For stepping in like that."

"Sure. No problem."

"'Cause, like, my dad loves that TV. I mean, he really loves it. So thanks."

"It's what friends do," said Evan, turning to leave.

That caught him by surprise. He hadn't meant to say *that*. It was a little hard to think of Scott as a friend after everything that had happened. But— where were they? He and Scott? Not friends. But not enemies. Somewhere between. Someplace that didn't have a name, or even any rules.

Evan scratched the back of his neck. "So, you know, I'm sorry," he said. "I'm sorry about the basketball game yesterday and the trial and everything. Look, you say you didn't take the money, and that means you didn't take the money. And I'm sorry I made such a big deal out of it and that I was such a jerk."

Scott nodded his head once. "Yeah, well, forget about the Morning Meeting thing. You know, you and Jessie apologizing. Because—well, just forget about it."

Okay. Evan felt better. He felt better than he had all week. It was like he'd been carrying a backpack full of rocks for days and days, but now he felt so light, he could practically fly. And man, was he *hun-*

gry. He could hear the chocolate chip cookies calling to him from all the way down the street.

Scott still looked pretty miserable, though, so Evan just said "See ya" and turned to leave.

He was at the top of the stairs when Scott called out, "Hang on." Evan turned and watched as Scott reached into his pocket and pulled out a key, then used it to unlock the file cabinet in the corner. Evan hoped he was going to offer him a Yodel for the road. A Yodel would taste pretty good right now.

But it wasn't a Yodel that Scott pulled out of the file cabinet. It was an envelope, and Evan recognized it right away.

It was Jessie's envelope. The one that had $208 in it.

Scott handed it to him. "I'm sorry I stole your money."

Evan took the fat envelope. He'd forgotten what a thick wad the $208 was. All that work. All that sweat. Mixing the lemonade and hauling it all over town and standing in the hot summer sun. And then having to tell Jessie that he'd lost the money. That had been the worst part of all.

"I guess you're pretty mad, huh?" said Scott.

Evan was surprised to hear himself say, "No." And surprised to know that he meant it. Maybe it was the crummy trial or the nasty basketball game or the fact that he hadn't eaten anything in nearly twenty-four hours. Whatever it was, Evan felt emptied out. There just wasn't any anger left inside him.

"Why'd you take it, though?" he asked, looking at the money.

Scott shrugged. "I don't know. 'Cause you had it, I guess."

"Oh," said Evan. That didn't make sense to him. It's not like Scott needed the money. After all, his parents bought him everything he wanted: the newest iPod, the best hockey skates, the biggest TV. It just didn't make sense to Evan.

But some things never do.

"I gotta go," Evan said, stuffing the envelope into the front of his shorts. The sun was low in the sky, and his mother didn't let him ride his bike after dark. Soon, he'd go over to Adam's house for the big meal that marked the end of the Day of Atonement. "See you," he said to Scott.

"Yeah, later." They both walked out into the front yard, then Evan climbed on his bike.

"Hey!" shouted Evan as he pedaled down the driveway. "The next time a ball goes over the fence, it's got *your* name on it. You owe me for that!"

Evan didn't stick around to hear Scott's reply. It would come up again—the ball in the swamp—the next time they were messing around on the basketball court.

Solemn Pact of Silence

This contract is <u>legal</u> and <u>binding</u> for all parties who sign below.

The undersigned do solemnly swear to never reveal to the members of classroom 4-O, or to any adults who might ask questions, what really happened to the two hundred and eight dollars that went missing from Evan Treski's shorts pocket on September 5th.

This matter is considered closed, now and forever, and the details of it will be sealed for all time.

Evan Treski

Jessie Treski

Scott Spencer